'You are o
pointed out.

'Not now,' Matt sa quietly. 'I'm officially engaged as your locum.'

She remained silent as they walked, wondering why she felt so confused towards this young man. At thirty he was five years younger than her and though the age difference should not affect her the way it appeared to, was it the reason, she asked herself with painful honesty, why she felt so uncomfortable in his presence? Did his youth and vitality disturb her that much? Or was it the emotions that he appeared to evoke in her, emotions that she hadn't felt since long before Sean died and which she was reluctant to experience again?

Carol Wood lives with her artist husband, her grown-up family and parents on the south coast of England. She has always taken an interest in medical matters, especially general practice and nursing in the community. Her hobbies are walking by the sea and watching wildlife, and, of course, reading and writing romantic fiction.

Recent titles by the same author:

TIME ENOUGH
A LITTLE IMMEDIATE CARE
SOMETHING SPECIAL

HEAVEN SENT

BY
CAROL WOOD

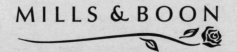

MILLS & BOON

All the characters in this book have no existence outside the imagination of the author, and have no relation whatsoever to anyone bearing the same name or names. They are not even distantly inspired by any individual known or unknown to the author, and all the incidents are pure invention.

First published in Great Britain 2000
Harlequin Mills & Boon Limited,
Eton House, 18-24 Paradise Road, Richmond, Surrey TW9 1SR

© Carol Wood 2000

ISBN 0 263 81918 3

Set in Times Roman 10½ on 12 pt.
03-0001-53006

Printed and bound in Spain
by Litografía Rosés S.A., Barcelona

CHAPTER ONE

IT WAS half past twelve by the time Abbie finished signing the small pile of prescriptions that lay on her desk. As her afternoon surgery was not due to begin until two thirty she would spend her lunch-hour in the office, studying the proposals of the last practice meeting. Undisturbed, she could browse at leisure through the suggestions of the nursing staff for summer clinics.

As she was about to leave her room the internal phone rang and, somewhat reluctantly, she returned to answer it.

'Someone on line one for you, Dr Ashby,' said Rachel Brompton, the receptionist on duty. 'He's not a patient, says his name is Carrig. It's a bad connection, I'm afraid. He's probably on a mobile.'

'All right, put him through, Rachel. And will you leave the office open for me? I'll be using it during my lunch hour.'

'Ok, Dr Ashby. Here you go.'

'Dr Ashby here.' Abbie winced at the static on the line and she held the receiver away from her ear.

'Dr Ashby, my name is…' The voice disintegrated, and a loud whistling caused Abbie to remove the phone from her ear once more. 'Sorry about the interference,' the voice continued, as they were reconnected. 'I'm phoning on behalf of your sister, Joely.'

Abbie's heart lurched as she gripped the telephone. 'Joely?' she repeated sharply.

'Michele had a small accident this morning. She fell backwards from her swing and knocked herself out for a few moments.'

5

Fear clutched at Abbie's heart at the mention of Michele, her sister's four-year-old daughter. 'What happened?' she demanded, her fingers gripping the telephone tightly. 'Is she conscious?'

'Yes, she's conscious. However, we've called for an ambulance just to be on the safe side. I'm sure it isn't serious…' The line broke up again, and despite Abbie's attempts to recall the man's voice there was an ominous buzzing on the end of the line.

She hung up, her heart pounding. Closing her eyes for a moment as she took a deep breath, she tried to remember exactly what the man named Carrig had said. Whoever he was, he had explained that the fall wasn't serious and that Michele was conscious, but who was he and how did *he* know if it was serious or not?

Abbie tried to control the accelerating panic inside her, reminding herself that Joely's house was just a short distance away and that she could be there in no time at all. Grabbing her case, she hurried into Reception, where Rachel was tidying the magazines.

'Michele's had a fall,' Abbie said hurriedly. 'I'm going over to the cottage straight away.'

'Michele?' The receptionist looked shocked. 'Is she all right? What happened?'

'I don't know the details,' Abbie said as she fled towards the outer doors. 'I'll let you know if I'm going to be delayed.'

'Drive carefully,' she heard the receptionist shout, but by the time she had reached her red Fiesta, unlocked it and started the engine, one glance in the driving mirror reflected the fear that had tied her stomach into a tight knot.

The two-mile journey across the Lakeland town of Rendale felt like twenty as each bus, car and even bike seemed to block her path. At last she turned the corner of the road her sister lived in and drew her car to a halt outside the pretty semi-detached cottage. As she climbed out of the car a tall, dark-haired young man appeared at the side of the house and hurried towards her.

'I'm Matt Carrig,' he greeted her as they met halfway across the pocket-sized front lawn. 'Dr Ashby?'

'Yes,' Abbie answered at once. 'Where is my niece?'

'We haven't moved her,' he assured her as they turned to hurry along the path that bordered the house. 'She's in the back garden with Joely.'

'What happened?' Abbie heard herself demanding. 'Where is the ambulance? Did you say you'd rung for one?'

'It should be here soon. As I said, it was a fall from the swing. She hit her head on the concrete foundation and there was a slight impairment of consciousness for a few seconds.'

Abbie glanced apprehensively at the stranger, who seemed to be making light of what might be a potentially serious situation, but as they rounded the side of the house Abbie forgot about the man accompanying her as she saw her niece's tiny body, lying prone on the ground by her swing.

Joely looked up from where she was kneeling beside Michele. 'Abbie, I didn't know whether to ring you or not,' she said shakily. 'I couldn't think what to do first.'

'Of course you should have rung me,' Abbie replied as she knelt beside her sister. Abbie looked down at her niece. 'Hello, mischief, what have you been up to?'

Dressed in pink dungarees and transparent Cinderella sandals, Michele gave Abbie a wobbly smile. 'H-hello, Aunt Abbie.'

Abbie took Michele's hand, relieved to discover it was warm and each finger flexed as she squeezed them. 'How do you feel?'

'A bit sick,' her niece replied. 'I fell off my swing and hurt my head.'

'She was out cold for a few seconds,' said a young man who was kneeling on the other side of Michele. Abbie recognised him as Phil Sheppey, Joely's next-door neighbour. 'I was in the house with Joely, trying to sort out the washing machine. But luckily Matt saw what happened and vaulted the fence to get to her.'

'It was, literally, only a few seconds,' said the man she now knew to be Matt Carrig. She frowned up at him as he spoke, his dark brown eyes calmly meeting hers.

'Did you move her?' Abbie demanded at once, hearing the abruptness in her voice but unable to do anything about it.

'No,' he told her quietly. 'I didn't.'

'It all happened so quickly,' her sister broke in. 'One minute she was playing on her swing, the next she was flat on her back on the ground.'

Abbie glanced at the man who had rung her on the mobile, remembering that Joely had not yet been connected to a land-line and that her sister must have given him the mobile to use.

Assuming that he must be a friend of Joely's neighbour, Abbie gave him a brief nod as he sank to his haunches beside her. 'She's responsive in all four limbs,' he told her, smiling at Michele as he spoke, 'so we've no worries there, but certainly that lump on the back of her head will need looking at.'

At that moment the ambulance siren sounded close by and very soon Phil was guiding the two paramedics into the back garden. Michele didn't complain as a support collar was gently wrapped around her neck and she was transferred to the ambulance by stretcher.

'Are you coming with us?' Joely asked as they waited at the ambulance. 'You have surgery, don't you, this afternoon?'

'Yes, but not until two-thirty.' Abbie hesitated, feeling that she should accompany her sister.

'Do you want me to phone in and see if I can get a few hours off from work?' Phil offered as the paramedic waited to close the doors.

'No, I'll be all right, 'Joely said though Abbie saw that her hands were shaking.

'Perhaps I can be of help,' Matt Carrig said suddenly. 'I'll drive to your surgery, Dr Ashby, and explain what's happened. I'm sure the reception staff will sort something out in your absence. Hopefully, Michele's X-rays won't take too long. You may well be back in time.'

For the first time Abbie noticed Matt Carrig's appearance as he gazed down at her with warm, liquid brown eyes. A thatch of unruly dark hair appeared to be wildly at odds with his calm, dark gaze. He was tall and athletic-looking and seemed completely at ease in her sister's garden, making Abbie wonder for one brief second if he could perhaps be the new man in Joely's life.

'Mummy! Aunt Abbie!' Michele wailed from the ambulance as the paramedic began to close the doors.

'Go with your niece and don't worry about the surgery,' Matt Carrig said, sliding his hand under her arm. Before Abbie could think what was happening, she was following Joely up into the ambulance and the doors were closing behind her.

A few seconds later they were on their way, with the siren wailing above them. Michele looked over the top of her collar with anxious eyes. 'Aunt Abbie, you will stay with us, won't you?'

'Of course I will, darling,' Abbie assured her, leaning across to hold her hand.

'What's going to happen at the hospital?' Michele asked tearfully.

'You're just going to have some photographs taken, that's all.'

'Will it hurt?'

Abbie shook her head. 'Not a bit.'

Joely bent forward and kissed her daughter's forehead, brushing the damp hair from her eyes. 'We'll be with you all the time, darling.'

'Thanks for coming, Abs,' Joely said as she sat back and sighed. 'I didn't want to worry you but Matt said that you should be told.'

Abbie nodded. 'Of course I would have wanted to know. He was certainly right about that.'

A smile parted Joely's lips. 'Matt has the proverbial doctor's antenna. You all seem to be on the same wavelength when it comes to emergencies.'

'He's a doctor?' Abbie asked in surprise.

'Didn't I say?' Joely looked blank. 'Of course, you two haven't met before, have you? Matt's from Australia.'

'Australia?' Abbie shrugged. 'I didn't notice an accent.'

'No, that's because he's English by birth. His family emigrated there when he was in his teens. Phil and Matt were in training together and Matt's spending some time with him before he goes back to Aussie in the autumn.'

'But Phil's not a doctor, is he?' Abbie said, trying to bring to mind the little she knew of her sister's new neighbour.

'No, Phil never got through his second year,' Joely explained. 'He went into journalism and he's now working on one of the Carlisle rags.'

'Oh.' Abbie nodded and saw that Joely was smiling.

'And for your further information he's divorced, he travels a lot and, er, he's a really nice guy,' Joely added, her grin widening.

Joely always found their conversations regarding men amusing, and Abbie tried not to let her concern for her younger sister show through. Joely had been living at the cottage since Christmas and it was to be expected that she would meet new friends and neighbours. Since leaving the family home and taking up life as a single parent, Joely had certainly begun to spread her wings.

Abbie glanced at her sister as Joely leaned forward to draw the blanket over Michele's chest. Joely was as fair as she herself was dark, Joely following in their mother's footsteps whilst she herself had the thick brown hair and emerald green eyes of their father. They had never been taken for sisters—Joely was a chatterbox, Abbie more of a listener. Joely had arrived late in their parents' lives, a decade after Abbie, and Abbie could remember clearly her baby sister's noisy entrance into the world.

Little Michele was a carbon copy of her mother. Abbie adored her, perhaps too much sometimes, her affection for her niece filling the gap in her life that motherhood had not.

'Tell Aunt Abbie 'bout the bobickuw,' Michele suddenly said with a giggle. 'You know, what Uncle Phil said.'

Joely laughed. 'Not that we'll be going now, mischief, not after today.'

'What's a bobickew?' asked Abbie curiously.

Michele and Joely laughed. 'Phil asked us to a *barbecue* this evening,' Joely explained, winking at her four-year-old daughter. 'Matt was putting up the gazebo in the garden when he saw Michele fall. He's nice, isn't he?'

Abbie blushed, knowing that her sister could always read her mind, and at that moment the memory of the tall, dark-haired stranger had flashed through her mind. She rested back against the padded seat, painfully aware of her sister's amusement. She realised she must sound like an old mother hen and she decided not to say another word on the subject of the two good-looking males that seemed to have suddenly appeared in her sister's life.

She had to admit Joely was blooming these days—could either of her neighbours be the cause of this? She certainly hoped it wasn't the Australian who had captured Joely's attention. It was accepted that holiday romances were short-lived and, sadly, little Michele was the result of just such a relationship. Putting the unpalatable thought to the back of her mind, she took comfort from the fact that Michele had never lacked in love and seemed to have an abundance of self-confidence.

'We're here,' said Joely beside her, and Abbie glanced out of the rear window to see that they had arrived in the grounds of Rendale Cottage Hospital.

The A and E duty doctor confirmed the need for X-rays and admitted Michele for one night's observation. Joely decided to stay at the hospital too, and Abbie finally left the ward at a quarter past four.

She caught a taxi back to the cottage and collected her car, her thoughts straying back to her niece as she drove to the surgery. Michele was going to be all right as far as they knew.

'Abbie, stop worrying!' Joely had laughed when Abbie had reluctantly said goodbye as Michele had been transferred to the ward. 'Accidents happen all the time with children. You know that—you've treated dozens of kids over the years.'

Abbie thought how true that was. But Michele was young and vulnerable—and fatherless. Having no role model, that was the factor she worried about most. It had been different for her and Joely. Their father had been a hero of the village of Rendale. It was said that Dr Bob Burchfield had cured all ills, a much-loved man who had maintained traditional values and had been loved more for his character than his expertise. Sean, her late husband, had also been regarded highly.

The two men had been partners at the practice she had

inherited, and had the tragic accident at Esk Fell five years before not claimed both their lives, Michele would have still had a loving grandfather and a caring uncle.

Almost without realising it, Abbie found herself back at the surgery. Rachel, at the desk, greeted her with a smile. When explanations about Michele were over, Abbie glanced around the empty waiting room. 'Did Dr Carrig pass on my message?'

Rachel nodded. 'He talked to Dr Morgan, then took your surgery.'

Abbie stared at Rachel wondering if she'd heard correctly. 'He did *what*?'

'Dr Carrig offered to help out and Dr Morgan accepted. There wasn't a complaint to be heard from your patients, Dr Ashby. And you know what some of them are like.' Rachel suddenly flushed as her gaze travelled beyond Abbie's shoulder. 'Oh, Dr Carrig, I was just saying, we'd never have coped if it hadn't been for you taking Dr Ashby's surgery.'

Abbie looked from Rachel to Matt Carrig who came to stand beside them. 'You saw *all* my patients?'

'Could we talk?' he suggested, lowering his voice and gesturing towards her consulting room.

Abbie glanced at Rachel who seemed to be lost in a trance as she gazed up at the tall, handsome young man.

'I gather, from what I heard,' Matt Carrig said as he accompanied her along the hall, 'that Michele is staying in hospital for observation?'

She nodded as they walked into her room. 'Yes,' Abbie said through gritted teeth, trying to come to terms with the mixed emotions inside her caused by Matt Carrig. She met his gaze as she sat down behind her desk and he took the patient's chair. 'Why didn't you tell me that you were a doctor?' she asked immediately.

'I did tell you on the mobile,' he told her, shrugging. 'You couldn't have heard me through the interference.'

Abbie had that odd sensation again in the pit of her stomach and she moved uncomfortably in her chair. She was unable to decide whether she was grateful for his help with her patients or whether she resented his intrusion. One thing was for sure as she met his unswerving gaze. Her attempt to look unflustered fooled no one, least of all Matt Carrig. His large body seemed relaxed, long legs thrust out in front of him, one elbow propped casually on her desk.

'May I explain what happened when I arrived here?' he said as she finally met his gaze.

'Yes, I think you'd better.' She waited for him to continue.

'Mrs Kay,' he said quietly, 'your first patient, as I'm sure you know, was already with Dr Morgan when I walked into the surgery. At twenty-eight weeks into her pregnancy, Dr Morgan found her BP was high and there was noticeable oedema. He was concerned enough to admit her. He came out to Reception to ask one of the girls to ring her husband and that was when I introduced myself. Fortunately, Dr Morgan had read some of my papers on paediatrics, which at least was some proof of my identity.'

Abbie could not help but look surprised. 'I see,' she said, feeling herself begin to calm down.

'I offered to help with some of the emergencies that were swelling the waiting room and Dr Morgan accepted.'

'You also saw the remainder of my list?'

He nodded. 'Only because your receptionist had problems trying to book further appointments.'

Abbie raised her eyebrows. 'Well, I suppose we are in your debt, Dr Carrig.'

'Not at all. I'm sure you would have done the same,' he said with a ghost of a smile. 'Dr Morgan was inundated with holiday-makers from the Rendale Activity Centre. I could hardly leave while there was something I could do to help. And it's Matt, by the way.'

Abbie pushed the wing of glossy chestnut hair from her green eyes and returned his smile. 'We do seem to have a problem with the new centre. Their on-site clinic is not always supervised by a doctor and we seem to get the over-spill—' Her voice tailed off and for a few moments they were silent.

'There was someone by the name of David Carter who troubled me,' Matt Carrig said after a pause. 'He complained of palpitations, trembling and sweating, and found swallowing difficult. There was nothing physically wrong as far as I could see.'

'Is he a temporary resident?' Abbie asked.

'Yes, apparently so. From the little he told me he has a domestic problem on his hands. I did a simple relaxation technique with him and his swallowing improved. When I suggested that he might be suffering from a series of panic attacks, he said he may only be staying in Rendale for a short time and would consult a doctor when he returned home.'

While she tried to work out how she felt about Matt Carrig's obvious competence, he leaned back, stretched and drew the palm of his hand down the back of his head, a movement that caused his thick, dark hair to slide beneath the white collar of his rugby shirt. 'And then there was a man called Jasper Macdonald,' he said, frowning deeply.

'Did Jasper agree to see you?' Abbie asked in surprise.

He nodded. 'Yes. He wanted his usual prescription for arthritis, but then we began to chat. From your notes and from what he told me I gather his health is worrying you.'

Abbie nodded slowly. 'Yes, I'm afraid so.'

'You've asked him to go in for tests?'

Abbie shrugged. 'To no avail. At fifty-two he's a committed bachelor who has always been very fit, working as a hill guide.'

'And he refused the tests?'

'It was only by repeatedly phoning him to come in to see me today that he agreed to an appointment, which was why I was surprised he agreed to see someone else.'

'You suspect motor neurone, don't you?' he said quietly, and Abbie stared at him, aware that he, too, must have suspected the terminal disease.

'Until we know the results, nothing is certain.'

He refrained from commenting but she knew that he had seen and heard the evidence for himself. Motor neurone, degeneration of the nerves within the central nervous system that controlled muscular activity, was a cruel disease, wasting the muscles of its victim and resulting in all loss of mobility. Abbie turned away because she did not want this man to see the sadness in her eyes.

'I'm sorry to have confirmed what you thought,' he said softly. 'I can guess how painful this must be for you. I understand, from what Mr Macdonald said, that he is a close family friend.'

She cleared her throat and nodded. 'Jasper was a close friend of my father and of Frank. They fished and played golf together.' She took a breath and forced herself to continue. 'My husband Sean and my father were killed in a road accident five years ago. Jasper helped my family through. He's always been a great source of strength.'

Abbie broke off, emotion threatening to overtake her. She stood up and walked to the shelf in the room on which she kept a box of tissues. 'I...I'm sorry,' she apologised, keeping her face averted. Appalled she was behaving so badly, she spread her fingers across the empty shelf, her eyes misty and unfocused.

To her further embarrassment she found that not only did she appear to have a large white handkerchief in her hand, but a stranger's arm had reached out to press her head against the warm cloth of his rugby shirt.

CHAPTER TWO

ABBIE lifted her head from the comfortable place where her cheek had rested on Matt's chest and moved away.

'A few tears are always a good way of releasing emotion,' he said as she walked back to her desk.

'I think it was talking about Jasper and the accident.' She swallowed, discreetly smoothing the wet patches beneath her eyes and returning the handkerchief to him.

'When was the accident?' he asked her.

'Five years ago. My father and Sean were returning from a house call on Esk Fell. Sean was driving, the car skidded on ice and plunged over the hillside. Both Dad and Sean were killed outright.'

His voice was soft and she was conscious of his concerned gaze as he spoke again. 'It must have been very traumatic for you.'

She turned away briefly to compose herself, then, taking a breath, she asked, 'How long are you staying with Phil?'

'At least for a few weeks,' he explained. 'Don't hesitate to get in touch if you need me.' It was only then that she caught the faint Australian accent as he smiled before leaving.

Afterwards, she sat down and tried to piece together the events of the day as she cleared the last few items of correspondence on her desk. Feeling clearly at odds with herself, she decided to go home and take a shower before she phoned the hospital that night to find out how Joely and Michele were. Then she remembered her mother, with whom she lived in the big Burchfield family house. The news of Michele's accident would have to be broken to her, but perhaps by the time she returned from her day trip to Carlisle Joely might have telephoned with better news.

Rising from her desk, she picked up her case and car keys, glancing at the list of her patients who had all seen Matt that afternoon. She still found it difficult to accept the fact he seemed to have breezed effortlessly through their problems in her absence. Then she remembered the way he had looked at her and caused those odd sensations inside her, long-buried feelings which had caused her heart to race and her skin to flush.

Somehow she had felt like a girl again—ridiculous but true. Perhaps it was because she had buried those sensations so deeply after Sean's death that now they evoked such an irrational response in her. For a moment she was annoyed that Frank Morgan had been so swift to accept a stranger's help, then she berated herself silently.

Frank had shouldered Serena Kay's problems while she herself had chosen to accompany Michele to hospital. Serena, with her complicated history of miscarriages, was not an easy case to handle. She should have been here to see her, as she should have been here to talk to Jasper who, above everyone else, needed her support.

With a twinge of conscience, Abbie tucked the list in her drawer and closed it. How often did she have this battle with herself over who came first, family or work? After her father's death, Joely had fallen pregnant and her mother had become depressed. Life had changed irrevocably for them all as they'd tried to continue, and Abbie had shouldered both work and family responsibilities.

Five years on she was still battling with priorities. Today a stranger had appeared in her life, and for the first time in years, had relieved her of the pressures that she accepted without question.

As she left her room and closed the door she was forced to admit that there had been no complaints from patients or the staff. The only critic was her conscience, which in some odd way seemed to be tangled up with her troubled thoughts of Matt Carrig.

Two days later, on Saturday afternoon, Abbie sat in the conservatory of the large family home wondering how it was possible that she was actually considering the suggestion of Matt Carrig as locum to the practice.

Opposite her sat Frank Morgan on the large chintz sofa, and to her right Matt Carrig sprawled in the rattan armchair, his long legs encased in jeans and stretched out to cross at the ankles. His booted feet disappeared under the low coffee-table, which was covered in practice paraphernalia.

She had tried for the best part of the afternoon to avoid Matt's gaze and lowered her eyes to read the notes she had made concerning the emergency meeting.

Abbie still remembered Rachel's words when, the morning after Michele's accident, the young receptionist had breezed into her consulting room, her first comment an undoubted tribute to the young man opposite her now.

'Dr Carrig was *wonderful*,' Rachel had enthused. 'So good with all your patients—as if he'd known them for years. He must have a natural knack with people, don't you think?'

Abbie had shrugged, eager to study the paperwork before her. 'Yes, I suppose he must.'

'Dr Morgan says he specialises in paediatrics in Australia, that he's read some of his published articles. But…' Rachel had sighed dramatically '…it was those eyes that riveted me. My mum would call them "come to bed eyes" and, my goodness me, now I know what she means!'

Abbie swallowed as the notes she had made on the paper blurred in front of her eyes. She wasn't concentrating. Their agenda was a discussion of the unending flow of temporary resident appointments which had kept both Abbie and Frank tied to their rooms over the last few days.

'We shall have to set up some sort of independent surgery,' Frank had protested after another exhausting afternoon. 'We just can't cope, Abbie. With the success of the activity centre and the increase in tourists it would be unrealistic to think our summer lists won't double this year.'

Abbie had been forced to agree that Frank had been right. Rendale Activity Centre *was* a major tourist attraction, the facilities ranging from a dry ski slope to horse-riding. In addition, it offered residential courses in preferred sports and this had been given plenty of media hype over recent months. The new business had meant a tourist boom for both Rendale and neighbouring Hobcraig, but it had also meant added work for the surgery.

'So, I think we can count ourselves lucky that Matt has agreed to start straight away,' Frank was commenting, bringing Abbie back to the present and the minutes of the extraordinary meeting. 'You did say you're not due back in Adelaide until October, Matt?'

'I've decided to accept a post in general practice but not until November,' Matt explained sending a sharp glance in Abbie's direction. 'I expect to confirm a date, but it certainly won't be before October.'

'So October would suit you?' Frank said.

'Yes, perfectly.' Matt turned dark, quizzical eyes towards Abbie. 'If Abbie agrees?'

Abbie recalled how last night in her consulting room she had argued the point with Frank—was it wise to rush into engaging a locum? Patients preferred familiar faces, and they had managed last year to accommodate both holiday-makers and residents. Could they not cope again this year?

Frank, however, had been adamant. No one had protested on the afternoon of Michele's accident and the waiting

room had been clear by half past four. Eventually Abbie
had agreed reluctantly to the emergency meeting today.

Now the two men appeared to be waiting for her response. 'It has been hectic,' she acknowledged, 'and I agree
it's probably going to get worse during the summer. I'll
leave the decision to you, Frank.'

Her elderly partner nodded, his tired eyes filled with an
expression of relief. 'You know my feelings, Abbie.' He
smiled ruefully. 'With Matt's help I might squeeze in a few
rounds of golf while the weather's good.'

After that remark Abbie realised how much the pressure
must have been affecting her father's old friend. Golf was
his passion as it had been her father's. They had talked
constantly about the day when, after they'd retired, they
could improve on their handicaps. Sadly, that day had never
come.

At that moment, Bonnie Burchfield, Abbie's mother,
brought in a tray of tea and scones. She was tall and slender, like her eldest daughter, with the same deep green eyes.
'Welcome aboard, Matt,' she said, having overheard
Frank's last remark.

'I hope I'll prove useful,' Matt responded, as he flashed
another glance at Abbie.

'Since the activity centre opened the town has a completely new image,' Bonnie enthused. 'Rendale is definitely
a window of opportunity for the future.'

Abbie turned to look at her mother. She had a strong
feeling she had missed the point but calmly Bonnie poured
tea. 'Maybe I'll take up a hobby now that you have Matt
to help you, dear,' she added softly. 'In fact, I think I might
take that crash course in business studies that I mentioned
last week.'

Abbie vaguely remembered the brief conversation they'd
had regarding a new hobby, but she had paid little attention
to it.

'I've always thought how interesting it would be,' Bonnie continued, 'to run a shop.' She smiled at her astonished daughter. 'I've done very little since your father died, just cover at the surgery for members of the reception staff who are sick. I know for a fact that Stephanie would like more hours.'

'If your business skills prove as excellent as your cooking,' Matt said as he accepted one of the creamy scones, 'I'm sure you'll have every success.'

Half an hour later, Abbie excused herself from the meeting, explaining she had a visit to make. Once outside the house, however, she walked across the road and towards the nearby wood. Right now she needed its peace and tranquillity. Her mind seemed to be unable to grasp the fast-paced events of the past few days and she needed time to herself. She had just reached the shade of the trees when a movement beside her startled her.

Matt appeared by her side, looking lean and fit in his jeans and rugby sweatshirt, dressed entirely appropriately for a Saturday afternoon, she reflected, unlike her own tailored jacket and pencil-slim skirt worn for surgery that morning.

'Is this the route to your house call?' he asked as she continued to walk.

'No,' she was forced to acknowledge, knowing that he had guessed her motive for leaving the meeting.

'Would you object to some company?' he asked.

She shrugged. 'It's very quiet in the wood,' she said, slightly increasing her pace. 'I'm afraid you won't find much excitement in Rendale.'

'Is that what you think I'm looking for—excitement?' His tone was surprised.

'You are on holiday,' she pointed out.

'Not now,' he said quietly. 'I'm officially engaged as your locum.'

She remained silent as they walked, wondering why she felt so confused towards this young man. At thirty he was five years younger than her and though the age difference should not affect her the way it appeared to, was it the reason, she asked herself with painful honesty, why she felt so uncomfortable in his presence? Did his youth and vitality disturb her that much? Or was it the emotions that he appeared to evoke in her, emotions that she hadn't felt since long before Sean died and which she was reluctant to experience again?

'Have I done something to upset you?' he asked quietly, his dark eyes studying her profile.

Abbie stopped walking and turned to look at him, taking a deep breath as she did so. 'Matt, I don't want to appear unfriendly...'

'Don't you?' His mouth twisted into a grim smile. 'I'm afraid that's not the impression I'm receiving.'

'Then I apologise,' Abbie remarked guardedly. 'It's just that I've been used to working with Frank, flat out sometimes, and I see no real reason to change—'

'But obviously Frank felt the pressure,' he reminded her sharply. 'Even if you think you didn't.'

'It's a pressure I enjoy and respond to,' she answered, wondering why she was having to justify herself. 'Frank and I have managed to cope with a nucleus of patients in five years and from time to time have had locums for a few weeks or a day here and there. But I feel that asking you stay until October is—'

'Unnecessary?' He crooked a black eyebrow.

She hesitated as she sought words which would not offend. 'It's not that I'm ungrateful for your help.'

'Yet you would prefer it if you could continue as you were?'

'Obviously Frank feels the need for help,' she answered

evasively. 'I had no idea that he was so tired. Until today I hadn't realised that he was so exhausted.'

'Perhaps, then, it's the appropriate time for change?' He paused, as he, too, seemed to be thinking carefully of his response.

She looked back at him and saw that his forehead was creased in a deep frown but that, despite her attitude, he stood where he was, apparently unwilling to depart.

In the cool glade of the wood, the light reflected down on them between the spring leaves, and the scent of moss and undergrowth was all around. The soft breeze lifted her hair and blew it softly around her face as the leaves rustled on the trees.

Perhaps it was spring, Abbie thought for a moment, suddenly needing to move away as those feelings threatened to return again as she looked up into the dark, steady eyes that gazed down on her.

'There is something—' she began, and paused as he nodded slowly for her to continue. 'You must have reasons of your own for deciding to work with us. Wasn't this trip to England designed for holiday purposes?' It was a few seconds before he answered and she waited, wondering what his reply would be.

'As I explained, I have been offered a position in general practice and when I go home I intend to take it up. The next few months will be good experience for me. And Phil has made it clear that I'm welcome to stay. Obviously it's good to see him again. We've a lot to catch up on.'

Abbie nodded, knowing that his explanation should resolve her doubts and that it was clear the arrangement was mutually beneficial. However, the feeling that events had happened rather too swiftly and that she seemed to have little control over what was happening, still irritated her.

She did not let this show, though, as she nodded, and together they resumed their walk through the wood. Their conversation turned towards more practical matters regarding the surgery, and by the time they had completed a full circle and arrived back at the road, the arrangements for the following week were complete.

On Monday Abbie arrived later than usual at the tiny brick-built Cumbrian surgery in Witty Street. Frank had already acquainted Matt with the routine and Betty Trowbridge, the practice nurse, and Penny Moore, the receptionist on duty, were debating between themselves who would make the doctors' coffees.

Abbie could see that the young Australian had given them a pleasant shock. She smiled to herself as she walked past the confusion and into her room. Matt Carrig had certainly caused ripples on the surface of Rendale's small pond!

Waiting for her were Joely and Michele. 'How is that bump of yours, mischief?' Abbie opened her arms and Michele ran into them, apparently none the worse from last week's excitement.

'It's all better now, Aunt Abbie. We've got a present for you. Look.' Michele pointed to a shiny red box on her desk.

Abbie hugged her niece. 'But it isn't my birthday!'

Michele giggled. 'It's a thank-you present. From Mummy and me.'

Abbie took Michele's hand and led her towards the parcel. 'Shall I open it now?'

Joely shook her head. 'No, open it after surgery, when you've more time. Anyway, we've got to go to school now.'

'Oh, Mummy,' protested Michele, 'can't we open it now?'

Joely ruffled her daughter's hair. 'We don't want Aunt Abbie scoffing chocolates all through her surgery, now, do we?'

'But it isn't chocolates, Mummy, it's—' Michele stopped and blushed, having almost blurted out their surprise.

'Thank you, darling.' Abbie bent to kiss her niece.

'Come on, school-time!' called Joely, catching her daughter's hand and leading her to the door.

Abbie watched them disappear with the pang of protective affection that she always experienced when gazing at her sister and her child. The independent life seemed to suit Joely who was much happier since her move from the family home to the tiny rented cottage near the town centre.

Single parent status, though often the popular choice, had not been Joely's preference, rather the result of a brief affair that had resulted, Abbie believed, as a symptom of the shock of the accident which had killed Sean and her father. Up until then Joely had been a happy-go-lucky teenager. Five years later, she was in her mid-twenties and had learned a lot about life the hard way, as they all had since their tragic bereavement.

'Looks interesting,' said a voice, and Abbie came out of her thoughts to find Matt standing at the door, watching her.

As usual, she felt self-conscious under his scrutiny. 'It's supposed to be a secret,' Abbie told him. 'I'm not to open it until after surgery.'

He raised dark eyebrows and, though he did not comment, Abbie felt impelled to go on. 'It's from Michele and Joely,' she found herself explaining, then realised that her eyes were going curiously over the man standing on the threshold of her room. She frowned. 'Is there something different…?' she began, frowning at his crisp white shirt and smooth dark hair.

'I had a friendly sheep shearer attend to the problem of a haircut,' he said with a sudden smile.

'Obviously we have some very fashionable sheep here in Cumbria,' she responded solemnly.

They were both smiling as Penny appeared, and Matt stepped back in order to allow her to pass. 'Two early catastrophes from the activity centre,' Penny explained, handing Abbie the notes. 'And Serena Kay's husband is here.'

'I'll see Graham first,' Abbie decided immediately. 'Perhaps Dr Carrig can continue with the temporary residents.'

Penny nodded and glanced at Matt on her way out. 'Are you ready to start, Dr Carrig?' she asked.

'Yes,' he said and gave her a smile which Abbie knew must have sent Penny scurrying out to Reception with a blush on her cheeks. As she settled herself at her desk, she didn't know whether to be amused or distracted, for she, too, had experienced the same pleasure when the new member of staff had parted those full lips and revealed a smile that could not have failed to affect any woman who had witnessed it.

Fortunately the arrival of Graham Kay soon returned her thoughts to a practical level as the worried-looking man took a seat at her desk.

'How is Serena?' Abbie asked after initial salutations.

'Bed-resting on doctor's orders.' Graham Kay made an attempt to smile. 'She'll hate that, though, having to lie still all the time.'

Abbie had known Serena and her husband for years and had witnessed the unhappy string of miscarriages that his wife had suffered. Now in their late thirties, the couple felt that time was running out and that this pregnancy would be their last chance.

'What I want to know is whether the baby will be born healthy?' he asked with a frown. 'That is, if Serena manages to go full term?'

'The scans are all fine,' Abbie reassured him as she glanced through Serena's hospital reports. 'At the moment, Graham, all I can suggest is that you try to reassure her.'

'Some hope!' Graham Kay exclaimed mildly. 'Even scans don't reassure my wife.'

'What if I call in to see her later in the week?' Abbie suggested.

An expression of relief crossed his face. 'Oh, yes. Would you?'

'Of course, Graham.' Abbie knew how desperately the Kays wanted this baby, and after a brief chat with Graham she made a note to visit Serena over the Easter break.

After Graham Kay departed Abbie saw the usual assortment of Monday morning patients. Sore throats, earaches, migraines and chesty coughs were abundant and she wondered how Matt was coping next door.

Several locums had occupied her father's room since his death but none had elected to remain in Rendale. A female doctor had seemed the most enthusiastic but she had eventually married and moved south. For the past year they had managed with the help of Bob Wesley, the only other doctor in the vicinity.

At lunchtime Abbie noticed Matt's signature written against two names in the visiting book and she asked Penny about this.

'He's taken a map with him,' Penny told her. 'Said he wanted to get to know Rendale intimately.'

They exchanged rueful smiles and Abbie spent her lunch-hour with Frank in the staffroom. Oak-beamed and stone paved, the room had French windows which led through to a garden. Her father had created the little oasis and Abbie had set a simple brass plaque in the rockery to his memory. She loved to pause here, to take stock. Sean and her father felt closest when she was alone in the quiet setting.

After lunch she began afternoon surgery, relieved and saddened to see Jasper Macdonald who looked thinner and very gaunt despite the cheerful smile he managed to give her.

'I've arranged some tests,' she began firmly, hoping to avoid any argument this time regarding his treatment. But Jasper, as usual, had his own ideas.

'Not possible, Abbie. I've a party of walkers on Easter Saturday. I'll be busy all week with them.'

'But this is important,' she persisted, knowing he was probably using his work as an excuse, 'if we are to find out what's wrong with you.'

'After the holiday,' he finally agreed. 'I'll have them then and that's a promise.'

'How is the cramp?' she asked, referring to his latest symptom, one which she had noted on his last visit. She saw that his fingers were stiff as he flexed them and quickly removed them from the surface of her desk.

'Just old age.' He smiled. 'Nothing that bothers me.'

'Why not take some time off?' she suggested easily, not wanting to alarm him further but intent on trying to find a way to help him. 'How long is it since you had a holiday?'

He laughed, not his usual deep rumble, but a cracked, forced sound which was the result of a concerted effort to sound light-hearted. 'Come now, lassie. Stop trying to humour me and just give me something to take the edge of the aches and pains, won't you?'

She sighed, knowing that he knew her too well to argue the point. 'All right, I'll give you a repeat prescription for some painkillers, though only a few as you had a week's supply from Dr Carrig.'

'Women,' he grumbled as he pushed the prescription into his pocket. As he got up to leave he hesitated. 'Good lad he seems to be, too.'

'Do you think so, Jasper?' she answered, hiding her smile.

'Could do a lot worse.'

'Yes, I suppose we could.'

'Married?'

'No,' she said firmly. 'And he's returning to Adelaide in October. This is a temporary arrangement only.'

'Well, then, we'll have to make the most of him while he's here,' he said with a chuckle.

A little later there was a tap at the door. 'Are you free?' asked Matt as he walked into the room.

'Yes, take a seat.' She inhaled the scent of the familiar, tangy aftershave that she was now beginning to associate with his presence, noting the disconcerting leap of her heart. 'How did your visits go?' she asked quickly.

He shifted his long legs into a comfortable position beneath her desk and shrugged. 'No problem, thanks. I saw a chap called Haskins. He has severe angina, worsened, naturally, by the cigars he smokes.'

Abbie nodded. 'He told me he smokes three a day, but I would say that's a conservative estimate.'

'He won't stop?'

'Not for very long.' Abbie shrugged. 'We've tried everything from bribery to patches but he soon loses interest. We've all had a go—Frank and Jackie, the district nurse, my father and Sean. But nothing worked.'

'That doesn't mean to say we shouldn't go on trying.' He raised an eyebrow. 'Have you any objection to me throwing in a few ideas?'

'No, but I wouldn't bank on success.'

Did he think they hadn't tried everything they could think of with Arthur Haskins? And if her father or Sean had never been able to persuade the pensioner to give up cigars, what chance had a stranger?

'You have a full list for the afternoon, I take it?' she asked, changing the subject.

He nodded, placing a computer printout on her desk. 'Five TRs, plus permanent patients.'

Abbie frowned as she looked down the list and noted that she recognised few of the names, indicating that the summer was well on its way in Rendale. 'And it's Easter next week,' she added. 'I'm afraid after that the temporary list will double.'

'Which is why I'm here.' He shrugged, apparently unconcerned. 'Frank suggested I set aside an hour during the morning for temporary residents and increase when necessary.'

'Yes, that's a good idea,' she agreed, rising to her feet in order to conclude their conversation. 'Speak to the girls on Reception. No doubt they'll be pleased to have extra appointments available.'

He rose and walked to the door, but, before opening it, he looked back and said with a frown, 'Talking of Easter, Phil is having a barbecue on Saturday—Joely said you'll be coming.'

Abbie hesitated, astonished that her sister had said such a thing. 'Did she? She hasn't mentioned it to me.'

'Will you be able to make it?'

'I'm not sure—I'll think about it.'

He looked at her for a few moments then grinned. 'You should try giving yourself some time off, you know. It might not be as bad as you think.'

She looked at him and was about to say that she found ample time to enjoy herself when she felt like it when he raised his eyebrows and added, 'In fact, you could quite possibly enjoy yourself. Who knows?'

'Coffee?' Penny asked at an opportune time as she appeared in the open doorway.

Matt just shook his head and smiled. 'But I think Dr Ashby might like one,' he murmured as he moved off, casting a last wry glance in Abbie's direction.

Abbie cleared her throat. 'Coffee…er…yes…thanks, Penny.' As the receptionist looked at her quizzically, Abbie's mind was far away, trying to work out what Matt Carrig had meant.

CHAPTER THREE

On Good Friday Abbie drove to Rendale Cottage Hospital.

Serena lay on her bed, with her dark hair pulled back in a plait. As Abbie appeared she struggled to lower her feet to the floor, but Abbie shook her head and pulled up a chair beside the bed.

'Don't get up, Serena. I'm pleased to see you resting for once.' Because it felt airless in the ward, despite the open windows, Abbie loosened the top button of her blouse as she made herself comfortable on the hospital chair.

'You look lovely,' Serena commented. 'What a pretty colour green. It's just the shade of your eyes.'

'Yes, the blouse is a gift from Michele.'

'How is she now?' Serena asked.

'None the worse for her fall, luckily.' Abbie smiled. 'But, more to the point, how are you?'

'Bored,' Serena admitted. 'And while I'm unoccupied my mind goes into overdrive and I keep wondering if the baby is going to be all right. Even on television or the radio you seem to hear so many dreadful things these days.'

'To set your mind at rest I'll ask Sister to speak to Mr Rago,' Abbie suggested after a few moment's thought. 'He'll probably have a few words with you on his next round.'

Serena looked doubtful. 'The consultants always seem so busy. I don't want to bother them unduly.'

'If he realises you're anxious, he'll make it a priority.'

Serena sighed. 'I just feel I'm doing more harm than good to the baby by lying here, worrying.'

34

'Try to think positively,' Abbie advised. 'You've read enough self-help books over the years to know that you've done everything you can to help this baby on its way.'

Serena smiled. 'It's putting it into practice that's the hard bit.'

They chatted for a while longer. Abbie stayed until Graham arrived, bringing with him yet more books and literature for Serena to absorb. Pausing to speak to the duty sister on her way out, Abbie explained that it would be helpful if Serena's consultant would reassure her on his next visit.

Finally making her last call to a patient with a minor stomach upset, Abbie returned home to find her mother talking to Joely on the phone.

'We're invited to a barbecue tomorrow,' her mother said over their evening meal. 'Sounds nice, doesn't it, darling?'

Aware that her mother was waiting for a response, Abbie shrugged and changed the subject, unwilling to commit herself, but the following morning the telephone rang and she picked it up, guessing it would be Joely.

'You are coming tonight?' Matt asked immediately, and Abbie found herself indecisive once more as he waited for her reply.

'I'll try.' She hesitated, wondering why she was making such an effort to avoid him as the poor man was probably only trying to be friendly.

'Do I take it that I can tell Phil your answer's in the affirmative?' He tried once more. 'I think he's trying to get some idea of numbers, that's all.'

'Well, yes, I suppose you can count us in,' she agreed, telling herself that it would be clearly unfriendly to make an excuse. Besides, she didn't want to disappoint her mother who had seemed eager to go.

Her first thought after replacing the phone was what she would wear. Despite thinking about it for the best part of the day, she had still arrived at no clear decision by the evening.

Frowning into her wardrobe she took out several pairs of jeans and matched them with tops. She tried them all on, teaming this and that and not really knowing why she decided against each article—only that for some reason she was being more critical than usual. Normally she would have worn jeans and have had done with it, but, casting each pair back onto the bed, she searched in her wardrobe once more.

Finally she settled on a dress that she had bought the previous year for Michele's third birthday party. Its thin straps and swirling skirt of pale pinks and greens was appropriate for a warm evening, and she decided if it wasn't right for the barbecue then she probably wouldn't wear it at all this season.

For Michele's party she had matched the dress with flat black pumps but tonight she chose fashionable plum pink mules that matched the more vivid qualities of the pattern.

Her hair was no problem, she reflected thankfully as she washed it, styling it afterwards into a bob that fell easily onto her shoulders. The auburn lights in it were vivid and the sun had already been at work on the colour and texture so that it looked shining and glossy as it fell thickly around her oval face.

The final touch came in the form of small jade green studs in copper shells that fitted snugly onto her ear lobes. These were her favourite earrings, nestling discreetly on her lobes, reflecting the deep green of her eyes. Spraying herself lightly with the perfume that she liked most, she gave one last twirl in front of her mirror, then walked along the hall to find her mother.

'What time did you tell Joely we'd be there?' Abbie called as she passed the bathroom and heard her mother running a bath. Normally Bonnie was well ahead of schedule, but as Abbie glanced at her wristwatch she frowned.

'Oh, didn't I tell you, darling? A friend rang this afternoon and I've decided to go out to the cinema instead,' Bonnie called above the flow of water. 'I'm sure no one will notice if I'm not there. You go and have a lovely time.'

'But, Mum…' Abbie began, then gave up as her voice was drowned by the portable radio in the bathroom.

Abbie sighed, went back to her bedroom and wondered if there was a chance of changing her mind at the last minute too. But unlike her mother, she felt obliged to go.

By the time Abbie arrived at the cottage the sound of music drifted from the back garden along with the noise of laughter. Matt opened the door before she knocked, grinning as he waved her in. He wore denim Bermudas and a Barrier Reef T-shirt. 'Hi, there,' he said as she entered.

'Aunt Abbie's here!' Michele cried out as she ran towards them, her thin legs all angles in their luminous green leggings. 'You look smashing, Aunt Abbie. You're wearing that dress you bought for my party!'

Abbie smiled self-consciously as Matt grinned and added his vocal appreciation to Michele's. Her niece grabbed her hand and tugged her through the narrow passage towards the party and the sound of music.

Joely waved Abbie over to a small group of people, most of whom Abbie recognised as her sister's friends. After introductions, the conversation flowed and drinks were served. Abbie found herself chatting and laughing, aware that every so often she would look up and catch Matt's gaze as he helped with the barbecue or handed out drinks.

The night wore on and Abbie found that she was enjoying herself much more than she had expected. When Michele scampered off to play with her friend, Lucy, Matt arrived beside her with a paper plate piled high with food.

'Is all this for me?' Abbie said, looking at the daunting amount on her plate.

'Joely said you could do with some nourishment,' he said with a grin. 'There's space on the wall for two—over there.'

They moved away from the noise and he gestured to a corner of the garden as yet unoccupied. Abbie sat down on the garden wall, balancing the plate on her knee. Matt perched beside her, his long, tanned legs stretched out in front of him.

'She seems to be none the worse for wear,' he remarked as he nodded toward Michele who was playing with Lucy. His arm brushed against Abbie's as they looked at the girls and Abbie swallowed, trying to pretend to herself that she was not disturbed by the way she was reacting to his presence.

'Yes, she seems fine now,' she agreed, returning her attention to the plate on her lap, tasting one of Joely's mince pies.

'Glad you came?' he asked, and she looked up, their eyes meeting again. 'I had the feeling you might change your mind.'

For a moment she held her breath as the music drifted from the house, a slow love song that made the night and the atmosphere seem suddenly very special. 'No, not me,' she said half-truthfully. 'But Mum cried off at the last moment.'

'Well, I'm glad you made it,' Matt said quietly. Then the noise of the music drowned out conversation and they sat eating, watching the dancing and Lucy and Michele having fun.

After they had finished their meal, he leaned across and said, 'Is there somewhere else we could go for a while? Somewhere we could talk without having to shout?'

Abbie smiled. 'Do I take it you're not a pop fan?'

He laughed. 'In small doses, it's great. But I'm approaching saturation point.'

She nodded. 'Me too. There's a local beauty spot nearby, a wood.'

'Sounds great to me.'

They slipped away through the side gate and no one appeared to notice. Abbie didn't realise they were holding hands until they reached the wood. It was dark and she could barely see his outline. But his voice was deep as they walked together, only the noise of their feet on the fallen leaves as they walked breaking the stillness.

'Do you miss Australia?' she asked, suddenly self-conscious of the awkward silence that had developed between them.

He smiled and nodded slowly. 'The odd thing is, when I'm back there I miss England. It's an odd sensation when you've spent approximately half of your life in each country.'

'It must be,' she murmured thoughtfully.

'The spring, for instance, is very special here. The trees, spring flowers, *wild* flowers, they're unique to this country. Where else but in England would you find a bluebell wood? Then there's the British sense of humour, country pubs, Yorkshire pudding and snow at Christmas.'

'That's a pretty long list.'

'There's more,' he added dryly. 'British theatre, frosty mornings, hedgerows, Bonfire Night and seaside rock.'

She arched an eyebrow. 'Oh, yes, that too.'

'And back in Adelaide there's the sun, the ocean, the surf, the wide spaces and the barbies. But somehow I suppose I always think of the Lakes as home.'

'You were born here?'

He nodded. 'I was seventeen when Dad emigrated. Just started college. He was a hill farmer and went out to farm in Australia.'

'Was that good or bad for you?' she asked curiously.

'A bit of both, I think. My brother settled easier. He's five years younger than me and he didn't leave behind so many friends.'

'Seventeen.' She sighed thoughtfully. 'A new country. A fresh start. It must have been exciting.'

'Yes, it was. We lived in Sydney at first. I trained at Sydney General, specialised in paediatrics and wrote a few articles. For some reason the powers that be thought they were worth publishing.' He shrugged. 'That about brings me up to date. What about you?' he asked quietly.

She shrugged. 'Five years ago I found myself with the practice to run and Mum and Joely to consider. Then there was Michele. After her birth, well, it seemed sensible for us to live at home with Mum until Joely decided to move last Christmas.'

His voice was soft as he said, 'But what about you? Have you never wanted to get married again?'

She looked down at her hands and automatically twisted the small diamond ring on her finger, the one Sean had given her on her eighteenth birthday. 'No,' she said quietly, 'I've never wanted to.'

She looked up at him, wondering why she was revealing so much about herself, but it seemed almost a natural process and she found herself continuing. 'There was never anyone but Sean. We grew up together, had the same things in common, we were good friends—that's not something I expect to find again in one lifetime.'

'But you're young,' he said softly. 'Your whole life is ahead of you, Abbie.' He lifted his hand and drew a finger under the wing of auburn hair that had fallen across her face. Gently he folded it behind her ear. 'You're young and very lovely. There is a future ahead of you. It can't be filled entirely by work.'

The minute seemed to go on for ever. His eyes held hers

in the darkness. The silence of the wood was uninterrupted. Her heart was beating very fast as she tried to take her breath. He took her in his arms and drew her close. Her hands seemed to run of their own accord over the strong shoulders above her.

'This is better,' he whispered. 'I've longed to do this all evening.'

'Have you?' she whispered, trembling.

'You'd better stop me now if you have any objections,' he said, tilting up her chin so their lips met.

She stood wordlessly, amazed she wanted his kiss so much. As his lips covered hers she felt their tell-tale stirring of desire at his touch. She was astounded by her response, her arms winding around his neck.

She reached up and touched his face and he slid his fingers into hers, kissing them lightly. 'You're going to tell me we shouldn't be here,' he said. 'That we shouldn't do this.'

'Was I?' she breathed.

'And I would answer you that, professional considerations aside, we are two unattached adults who have a healthy attraction towards one another.'

She gazed up into the dark shadows that were his eyes. 'No, you're wrong. I was going to say that it's been a long time since this has happened to me.'

'So I needn't have stayed awake all last night, rehearsing my argument?'

'Did you?'

'Oh, yes, Abbie. I've stayed awake a lot lately, thinking about you.' Before she could speak, he lowered his head and kissed her again, his tongue probing gently for her response.

This time there was nothing to distract her, just the adrenaline rushing into her veins. There seemed no part of her left untouched by his kiss, no patch of skin that did not

tremble at the depth of passion she felt. Seeking and enquiring, his kiss probed deeper, his hands holding her firmly
against him until at last he relaxed and set her free.

'Don't say anything,' he warned softly. 'I read in your
eyes whatever you think.'

'But you can't see my eyes,' she whispered.

'Yes, I can. The moon is my light. I can read everything
about you.' He bent to kiss her eyelids and she shivered.
His lips moved over her lashes and eyebrows this time, with
a desire that made her realise how much she wanted to kiss
him as she swayed against him and gave herself up to the
growing wonder of exploration.

'Do you want to go back?' he whispered at last.

'Is it late?' she murmured, not wanting to slide her arms
from his neck.

'Late enough for someone to notice, I suppose,' he said
on a soft sigh. 'As far as I'm concerned, we could stay here
all night.'

Abbie thought it was the most beautiful night she had
ever known. All of nature seemed to be present in the
wood. An owl hooted, a bat skimmed across their path. A
fox barked, calling to its mate hiding somewhere deeper in
the trees.

'Where have you been?' Joely wanted to know, as they
arrived at the cottage just as the party broke up.

'Walking,' Matt said, his eyes twinkling.

'Where is Michele?' Abbie realised it was much later
than she had thought.

'Crashed out on the sofa,' Joely said, and grinned. 'She
said to say goodnight.'

After the goodbyes, Abbie tiptoed into Phil's front room.
Michele slept on the sofa under a quilt, her blonde hair
fanned out over the cushion, her thumb in her mouth.

Joely crept up beside Abbie and poked her in the ribs.
'What have you two been up to?' she whispered.

'Oh, nothing,' Abbie replied with a poker face. She bent down to her slumbering niece and slid a lock of blonde hair from her forehead.

There was nothing really she could say—she hardly knew herself. The taste of Matt's kiss was still on her lips, the touch of his fingers lingered on her body.

Phil and Matt crept into the room. 'I'll carry Michele next door,' Phil said quietly.

In the final exodus, Abbie caught Joely's gaze. Unexpectedly, her sister smiled, as if she had guessed at Abbie's feelings.

'I think it's time I left too,' Abbie said as they followed Phil into the hall and out into the front garden.

'I'll walk you back home,' Matt said quietly.

The four of them stood outside in the moonlight and looked up at the sky. Michele stirred under her quilt and Phil moved towards the gate.

'Goodnight,' Phil and Joely called.

'Living next door has its advantages,' Abbie remarked as Matt slipped his sweater around her shoulders and reached for her hand.

'In Phil and Joely's case, yes,' he agreed.

They walked slowly, taking leisurely strides, not wanting a perfect evening to end.

'Does Michele ever see her father?' Matt asked.

'No, she doesn't.' Abbie paused. 'Michele was the result of a holiday romance. Joely never saw him again.'

'That must have been very hard for her.'

'Yes. She was recovering from Dad's death. But now none of us can imagine life without Michele.'

'And Phil?' Abbie asked. 'He's a friend from school, isn't he?'

Matt nodded as they neared Abbie's house. 'He married a local girl, but she left him for someone else. It's a pity, he's a nice guy.'

'Will you come in for coffee?' Abbie asked at the gate.

'Thanks, but it's late,' he declined, still holding her hand. 'I don't want to disturb the household.' They stood in the drive, two silhouettes outlined by the moonlight. It was a beautiful spring night and Abbie breathed it in.

'Thank you for a lovely evening,' she said.

'Will I see you again?'

She laughed softly. 'Of course. At the practice on Monday.'

He paused. 'I meant—like this.'

She felt a dart of alarm. Were events going too swiftly?

'Don't answer that,' he said easily. 'I don't want to be disappointed.'

With that he bent to kiss her, and somewhere in the distance an owl hooted and the magic of the night seemed endless as he broke away, touching her face briefly before walking away.

Was she disappointed or relieved that he had not accepted her offer? she asked herself as she unlocked the door and let herself into the quiet house. Only the reading lamp in the lounge remained on. Her mother had left a note beneath it. Hope you had a good time, darling. Sleep well.

As she climbed into bed, Abbie doubted that she would sleep well. Her mind, stimulated by talk of the past, was full of vivid pictures—her father, Sean and the young Joely with her sparkling green eyes. The eyes of youth.

And now Matt, on the edge of her thoughts. It was a long time before she closed her eyes but when she did, her last thought was of the wood and the silence and the way her body had felt when he'd kissed her.

On Monday Abbie was summoned to her first case of heat stroke. The young man had been canoeing on Ullswater and the sun had burnt his neck. He felt too ill to come into the surgery so Abbie made a house call.

She applied a cold compress, reduced his temperature and waited until his breathing and pulse were normal again. By the time she returned to the surgery Matt had dealt with the remainder of temporary residents.

'Hello,' he said as he stood at her door later in the day. They gazed at one another and for a moment Abbie felt the acceleration of her heartbeat that had happened before. 'Will you be here until late?' he asked.

She nodded as she looked at him. 'Yes. I think we should talk.'

'All right, this evening, then.' He smiled once more and then walked away and Abbie sat down, taking her breath. What was she going to say to him and what had she decided to do?

As it was, fate took a hand. Because she was on call and a house visit took precedence that evening, it was Friday before their paths crossed again.

Dave Carter, the sports coach from Rendale Activity Centre, appeared in Abbie's consulting room, and Abbie recognised the name as she welcomed him.

'I really wanted to see Dr Carrig,' he explained, 'but he's busy this morning.'

Abbie glanced at Dave Carter's notes. She remembered the brief conversation she had had with Matt regarding the panic attacks, though nothing was said of these as she examined his left eye, his present reason for coming.

'The eye's been sore for several days now,' he told her, 'and it doesn't look very healthy. I thought it would go away but, if anything, it's got worse.'

'Do you suffer from hay fever?' Abbie noted the tiny bloodshot blood vessels and the slightly dilated pupil.

'I used to. But I haven't had it for ages,' he told her with a shrug.

Abbie slipped on treatment gloves and cleaned the cloudy watery fluid that filled the lens of the eye. 'Allergic conjunctivitis can be relieved by eye drops,' she explained. 'I'll prescribe some for you but you must keep the eye clean. Make sure you don't transfer the infection from one eye to the other.' She disposed of the cleaning materials and threw her gloves into the bin. 'How do you feel otherwise?' she asked.

He shrugged. 'OK, I suppose. I'm still having those panic attacks, but…'' His voice petered out.

'Are you under any stress?' Abbie asked.

'A bit, but who isn't?' He did not seem to want to talk about it and stood up. 'I have to get back to the centre. Thanks for seeing me, Dr Ashby.'

After he had gone, she glanced at his notes again. Matt had suggested a follow-up appointment but had it not been for the eye problem she was doubtful whether Dave Carter would have come.

Matt appeared at her open door later in the day and, after glancing around to see whether she had patients or not, he walked in. 'Busy morning?' he asked.

She nodded. 'Yes, but come in.'

He entered, taking a seat by the desk. 'Did I see Dave Carter earlier?'

'Yes,' she answered, knowing that this might be the opportunity she had been waiting for. 'I wanted to speak to you about him.'

'How is he?' Matt asked as he leaned forward to frown at her.

'Well, this morning the trouble was conjunctivitis, though I felt there was something he wanted to say and didn't.'

He nodded thoughtfully, smoothing his palm over his dark hair. 'You know,' he murmured, 'changing the subject for a moment, I was wondering how a children's clinic would go down with our patients. What do you think?'

'A children's clinic?' She frowned. 'Why do you ask?'

'I've seen four youngsters today, all under ten—ear infections, hyperactive behaviour and an eight-year-old, who, I believe, is dyslexic. I'd like to see some of them on a regular basis. That gave me the idea. A clinic set aside for the under-tens.'

'But have you enough time?'

'I'm sure I can make some.'

She hesitated. 'You really think there is a call for a clinic like this?'

He nodded slowly. 'I'd like to give it a try. If it doesn't take off we can scrap the idea. There will be nothing lost.'

The immediate question bothering Abbie was who would carry it on after he left? She sat quietly, her thoughts on the future, reflecting that it was all very well for Matt to suggest new innovations but how would they be maintained, if successful, after his departure?

'You're thinking that I shan't be here long enough to warrant setting up an experimental project?' he guessed, correctly, as he studied her reaction.

She looked at him and nodded. 'Yes, to be honest, I was.'

'Well, it's up to you.' His dark eyes were guarded. 'I have the feeling that whatever suggestions I have at the moment, none of them are going to be well received. Going by what happened on Saturday, you are probably regretting ever having set eyes on me.'

Her heart raced in the familiar pattern as she looked up at him. 'No, but I wanted to set things straight.'

'I take it you regret what happened?'

She nodded, her cheeks flushed. 'Yes—and yet no.'

He quirked an eyebrow. 'I prefer the latter part.'

Just then Stephanie interrupted them. 'A late TR, Dr Carrig. A boy of twelve. It sounds like flu. Will you see him?'

Matt nodded. 'Yes, I'll be along in a second.'

When Stephanie had left he rose. As he walked slowly

to the door he glanced back, looking at her with the same puzzled expression of a few moments ago. She thought for a moment that he was about to continue where he had left off, then he shrugged and opened the door, before saying that he would see her later.

When he had gone she sat back in her seat, her shoulders drooping, wondering what he would have said had Stephanie not entered. Eventually deciding she would really rather not know, for Matt Carrig had unsettled her enough as it was, she gave herself a brisk mental shake, relieved her explanation was over and that now things could gradually get back to normal.

CHAPTER FOUR

'WHERE are you off to?' Abbie asked her mother on Saturday afternoon as Bonnie hurried down the stairs.

'I'm going out with a friend,' Bonnie Burchfield told her daughter as she smoothed down her dress and glanced in the hall mirror. 'Do I look all right?'

'You look lovely. Is that a new dress?'

'Well, yes. Fairly new.' Bonnie blushed as she turned to face Abbie. 'What about you, darling? Are you taking Michele to her dancing class?'

'Not today. They have a two-week break.'

'It's a pity to stay in on a such a lovely day.' Bonnie glanced out of the window. 'My friend said he'd pick me up about two or thereabouts.'

'He?' Abbie repeated in surprise. 'You mean you're not going out with Karen?'

'No,' Bonnie said and blushed again. 'You don't know Don. He's a new friend of mine. Someone I met on the computer course.'

Abbie's green eyes widened. 'Mum—you mean you have a date?'

Bonnie nodded. 'Actually, I've had a few of them.'

'But why haven't you said?' Abbie gasped.

'Oh, dear, look, there's the car—can I tell you about Don later when we both have more time?' Bonnie said hesitantly, hurrying to the door. 'Perhaps over coffee some time?'

A car horn sounded outside and Bonnie kissed her daughter then waved through the open door at a car parked outside the house. 'Must go, darling. See you later.' And with that she was gone, hurrying down the driveway to the gate to greet the occupant of the car who had already pushed the door open from the inside. Abbie watched it glide off, her eyes still glued to the shiny white vehicle as it sped away.

Just as Abbie was about to close the door another car pulled up. As she looked at it for some moments she realised it was Matt's hired car, a dark blue Citroën. Matt climbed out, dressed in chinos and a light-coloured linen shirt. He strode towards her, a smile touching his lips as he saw the surprised look on her face.

'Matt, what are you doing here?'

'I'm looking for a guide,' he said. Thrusting hands deeply into his pockets, he tilted his head to one side. 'I was wondering if you knew the way to Grassmere?'

For a moment she couldn't think what he meant and then as his eyes held hers, she said uncertainly, 'Why do you ask?'

He shrugged and turned to look up at the clear blue sky. 'A perfect day for…' He lifted his hand and brought it back to thrust it through his dark hair, then he turned back slowly to face her, adding on a sigh, 'I've been trying to think of a reason to ask you to come with me.'

'To Grassmere?' she said.

He nodded, the smile he gave her making her heart turn over as she realised his meaning. 'If I remember correctly, Grassmere is one of the prettiest lakes at this time of the year. And twice as nice if there's someone with you to share the view, of course.'

Abbie's smile was slow, and she knew that, much as the little warning voice inside her was telling her to refuse, she was about to ignore her own advice. 'I'll need to change,' she said, knowing that her protest was hardly worth the effort as he shrugged and told her that as far as he was concerned she looked just fine as she was.

'You look fantastic,' Matt said a short while later as she climbed into the car beside him, having quickly put on a simple peach sundress and strappy white sandals. There had been no time to do very much with her hair so she had just brushed it down onto her shoulders from the chignon that she had worn earlier that day.

'I should take you somewhere much grander to show you off,' he added, and Abbie smiled, disguising her nervousness by talking about work. Matt had seemed happy to go over the same ground, too, and mentioned having seen Jasper recently while he'd been out hill climbing with Phil. 'He was climbing higher than us,' he told her as they travelled along the Cumbrian lanes, 'but he seemed to be making his way with difficulty. I was in two minds whether to signal to him, but in the end I decided against it.'

'Was he with a group?' Abbie asked in concern.

'Not that I could see. We hung around for a bit and waited until he started his descent, but, even so, I don't think he should be climbing alone in his condition.'

She agreed, but what could she do to prevent him? It was a question that was still troubling her as they approached Grassmere and Matt slowed to contend with the traffic.

The café they stopped at for Cumbrian tea served delicious food on Lakeland pottery and they ate on a terrace, overlooking the lake. Abbie found herself telling Matt about her mother and the mysterious Don.

He showed no surprise at all. 'Good for her,' he said with genuine enthusiasm as they sat eating in the sunshine. Later, they strolled into town and Abbie bought a CD for Michele, and as the sun began to wane they made their way back to the lake.

They walked along the shore and found a quiet spot by the water's edge, stopping to rest on a natural platform of rocks. 'I used to come here and swim with Phil,' he said as they looked out over the water.

'What part of Cumbria are you from?' Abbie asked as he leaned back beside her, one elbow supporting him.

'Not Cumbria, just over the border,' he said with a faint smile. 'Coming down this way was a full day's journey for us. But in summer it was great. Usually we'd cycle and bring the tent.'

She rested back too, unconsciously keeping a space between them but in the soft evening sunshine she could still feel the warmth of his body reaching her, his familiar scent blowing across on the breeze and into her nostrils. 'Why did you decide to specialise in paediatrics?' she asked quietly, twisting a smooth blade of grass around her fingers as she spoke.

'I suppose because the opportunity arose in Australia and because I felt I had an aptitude for it.' He added after a while, 'What about you and Sean?'

'You mean why did we both stay in the Lakes to practise?' She had often wondered herself how it would have been if they had decided to move on and whether, in other circumstances, they would have started a family. 'I think because we took it for granted that Dad's practice suited us both. After our travels abroad with a charity organisation, Sean was eager to help Dad build up the practice. There were big changes in the health service at the time. Dad and Frank weren't young men any more. Dad wanted to retire and take Mum on a cruise somewhere.' She smiled reflectively. 'That had always been his dream.'

He was silent for a moment as he looked at her. 'And what's your dream, Abbie? What do you want from life?'

She shrugged, burying inside her the automatic response that lately had seemed further than ever from being fulfilled. She would be thirty-six next year. Despite her body clamouring for the one thing that she ached for, a child, she had begun to accept the fact that she would never be a mother. She had always thought that Sean would change his mind and share her dream of a big family, but somehow there had never been time in the early days. As the years had gone by, Sean had become more absorbed in the practice, sometimes to the exclusion of all else.

Dreams were a luxury Abbie had not indulged in since his death. Reality had meant that she was breadwinner and carer, her inner hopes and desires receding further than ever from realisation.

This thought made her unhappy and as usual she pushed it to the back of her mind, wanting only to remember the good parts of the years she and Sean had spent together.

'I have the practice,' she said eventually, 'and the family. There's never been time for very much more, I'm afraid.'

'But what do you want for yourself?' Matt persisted, his forehead creased deeply. 'There must be things you want. What about children of your own, for instance?'

His question startled her, for it had touched on the truth and the truth was something she had taken care to avoid since Sean's death. Determined to be supportive to Joely, her mother and Michele, and equally determined to make a success of the practice as her father and Sean would have wanted, she had come to terms with her life.

Now here was this stranger, posing questions that made her aware of the deep void in her life, demanding answers that she could not give while she continued to ignore her own needs.

She sat up and stared across the water, watching the smooth ripple of the tiny waves. She hesitated, then lowered her head as she spoke. 'It's a long time since I've thought about my dreams. I don't know if I have any now. I'm content. I live and work in a beautiful place, I have a family whom I love and who love me...' Her voice faded and she jumped when she felt his touch on her arm as he moved across the stone to sit beside her.

'Everyone should have a dream,' he told her as she looked up at him. The huskiness of his voice made her skin tremble as his fingers moved over her skin. 'Everyone needs to be loved. That's something that goes with being human, Abbie. Deny it and you'd be living a lie.'

'I'm not denying that's true,' she protested as she looked into his eyes. 'It just hasn't happened to me again after Sean.'

'Perhaps you haven't let it,' he said quietly. 'Perhaps you should try…' He bent his head towards her and she knew he was about to kiss her. 'Like this…'

She began to move away, her heart leaping as his breath fanned softly down on her face. 'Abbie,' he whispered, and suddenly she felt her body surrender, a wave of deep desire going through her as his lips covered hers and her eyes slowly closed.

He slid his arms around her waist and brought her towards him and she knew that the inevitable was happening and she could resist him no longer. As he kissed her, she saw through her lashes that the sun had melted behind the hills, spilling pink and golden rivers of colour across the sky.

His kiss was soft and enquiring, his lips exploring hers with gentle pressure until they drew her response, a response that left neither of them in any doubt as to how much she had wanted him to kiss her.

'Abbie…?' he whispered again, folding her into his arms and giving her no opportunity to answer as his body stiffened against her. She responded, opening her lips to his enquiry. A warmth filled the cold spaces inside her, bringing her alive as their kiss deepened. His arms closed around her and for a long while the kiss went on, her hands resting on his shoulders, her body arching against him.

Her heart beat so fast she felt its brief, powerful journey through her chest towards his, her sigh echoing the words he whispered against her cheek.

When he lifted himself away, he stroked her hair from her face. Sinking against him, she realised that words for the moment were redundant. She sighed again, the pressure of his body against her, his breathing in time with her own.

Abbie realised that she didn't want the day to end. Wishing that this moment could go on for ever, she refused to think of what would happen tomorrow, in what way their relationship might have changed or what she might have risked by allowing herself to feel these emotions. These were things she did not want to consider. Instead, an exquisite glow filled her as he drew her back to him, this time to kiss her with a passion that was equalled in intensity by her own.

When Abbie saw they were being watched, she realised she had not given the slightest thought to who might be in the area. She caught the movement out of the side of her eye and jumped.

She moved away as Matt, too, saw they had company. A young couple moved past them on the shingle and, exchanging brief smiles, Abbie blushed. She rearranged the strap of her sundress which had fallen from her shoulder.

'I thought we were alone,' Abbie said, making an effort to hide her embarrassment.

Matt reached out for her hand. 'Do you mind?'

She shook her head, smiling. 'No.' Then she laughed. 'It just felt like being back at school again.'

He looked at her and raised a quizzical eyebrow. 'Hasn't there been any time in your life to relax and let go?' He smiled as their eyes met.

'Not quite like this,' she admitted, 'but, then, I suppose I've had no desire to try.'

He nodded slowly, his frown melting away as his voice softened. 'So, Abbie, where do we go from here?'

It was a question she had been asking herself, and with no clear answer in her mind she was silent as his fingers entwined in hers and he sat back, his frown deepening again as he stared at her.

'I've no idea, Matt,' she responded quietly, 'but I do know that I haven't enjoyed myself quite so much in a long time.'

He seemed to think for a moment, on the point of saying something, then he looked back at the water. Suddenly he rose to his feet and, pulling her up beside him, he smiled. 'Come on. Don't let's waste a moment of this beautiful evening. Let's stroll around this bit of the lake and stop off for a drink before we go back home.'

She nodded. 'I'd like that.' Relieved that he had not forced the issue, she felt the warmth of his hand close over hers. They strolled in the magical evening, arms around each other's waists, talking of their lives and the things they seemed to have in common.

As they talked Abbie knew that something had changed in their relationship. Sooner or later she would have to confront the question of where this was leading her.

Bearing in mind that whatever happened between them, it could never be more than a brief affair, she wondered if she were crazy to consider the possibility of one. A few weeks ago she wouldn't have entertained the idea but now, with each passing day, she was getting to know him better. The physical attraction between them was strong, which didn't in itself change the facts. Matt was in the UK for a few months, that was all. When he returned to Australia in the autumn, there would come a natural conclusion to whatever relationship had developed between them. But why shouldn't she enjoy his company while he was here? It was, after all, as she had admitted herself today, a long time since she had relaxed like this.

It must not be forgotten, though, that she had feared Joely's involvement in such a relationship, not realising it was she herself who would be attracted to Matt. But, then, her sister, she knew, was looking for stability and security in her life. At twenty-five, Joely had her life before her and Michele to consider. Whoever she fell in love with would be faced with taking on a stepdaughter and Abbie knew Joely took this question seriously after all that had happened.

And herself?

Abbie realised she had posed an unanswerable question. As she had told Matt, after Sean's death she had kept busy with work and family. There had been few opportunities to socialise, and she'd immersed herself in the practice to such an extent that she had almost forgotten how it felt to walk along a beach on a soft, warm evening in the company of an attractive man. And not just any man. Matt Carrig was different. And that was what troubled her.

Her mind was revolving with questions as they walked. What was the harm in enjoying herself? Life was for living and she had done very little of this in a personal sense since Sean died. Perhaps it was time to pause for once. Why not have fun?

And as they talked long into the night over drinks at a waterside pub, Abbie was beginning to think she had little choice in the matter anyway.

Fate was taking a hand and, surprisingly, she was content for it to do so.

The following week brought an influx of holiday-makers to the small town of Rendale. Abbie saw that Matt dealt with the temporary residents smoothly and effectively. Arduous morning surgeries were never a problem to him, nor were the exhaustive lists of the hot afternoons or the time he took in getting to know the geography of the surrounding countryside.

A thrill of excitement gripped her when she saw him, though neither of them referred to their day at Grassmere. She did her best to keep a level head but, as her mother had remarked, she was looking radiant these days and people had noticed.

She had noted the same effect with pregnant mothers. When a woman was happy, it was reflected in her eyes, hair, body language and conversation. She felt as she hadn't felt in years. Her skin felt softer, her thick dark hair glossier, her body alive with a new sense of well-being.

At work, though, it was Jasper Macdonald who worried her. One morning he entered her room and wearily took a seat.

'I did as you said, lass,' he told her as he fought to recover his breath. 'Had those tests. They wanted me to stay in another week, but I refused. Can't abide being closed in like that, not able to get the fresh air or see the hills.'

He looked dreadful, Abbie thought. It was clear there had been a rapid decline in his heath.

'You must tell me what you suspect,' he said quietly. 'I would rather know than be left in the dark.'

'I can tell you nothing for sure—' she began, but he cut her short.

'I didn't hobnob with your father for years without gleaning a bit of knowledge,' he interrupted impatiently. 'Is it cancer?'

It was, she thought, characteristic of her father's old friend to be so forthright. It was time, she realised, to be frank in return, and to no great surprise of her patient she revealed her suspicions of motor neurone disease.

They talked for some time until, with a promise to return

the following week when they would assess the test results together, Jasper left.

She was still sitting in her chair deep in thought when Matt knocked and entered. 'You've just seen Jasper?' he said quietly.

She nodded and with a sigh explained what had happened.

'How did he take it?'

'It's difficult to say. I would have preferred to wait until I had the test results. It certainly isn't a foregone conclusion, but he wanted to know and I had to tell him what I suspect.'

Matt perched on the corner of her desk, one muscled thigh taking his weight, the other foot planted squarely on the floor. 'I'm afraid I haven't much better news for you. Reception has just had a call from Rendale Cottage Hospital. One of our temporary patients was admitted today, Dave Carter.'

'The sports coach with the panic attacks?'

He nodded. 'The hospital wants to know if we have any idea of his next of kin. All they found on him was our appointment card.'

Abbie looked puzzled. 'Have they tried Rendale Activity Centre?'

'I've no idea. They merely explained he's had an accident on his motorcycle. He's in Intensive Care.'

Abbie paused, frowning. 'Is he badly hurt?'

'He's unstable at the moment, with internal bleeding. The doctor asked for what medical information I had and I said I would call in on my way home. Do you want to come with me?'

'Yes, of course,' Abbie answered at once, aware that she had been last to talk to Dave Carter.

He nodded. 'We'll go in my car, if you like. Then I'll drop you back here afterwards.'

'All right. I finish at six tonight, barring emergencies.'

He looked at her for a few moments, his gaze meeting hers, then he rose slowly and walked to the door. The faint aroma of his cologne was left hanging in the air after he had gone, making her heart quicken as she inhaled.

Dave Carter's motorcycle was a write-off. The driver of the car had sustained only bumps and bruises and the hospital had discharged him.

'There's no spinal damage,' the ICU doctor told Matt and Abbie as they talked outside Dave Carter's room. 'He's drifting in and out of consciousness, but we're most concerned with the internal bleeding.'

They gazed through the transparent partition at an inert Dave Carter. Surrounded by an array of tubing and equipment, his face bore a line of stitches running from cheek to ear and his left arm was immobilised in plaster.

'Do you know anything of his history?' the doctor asked. 'Any clue would help.'

'Very little,' sighed Abbie. 'He's a temporary resident with the practice. I last treated him for an eye infection, and before that Dr Carrig saw him.'

Matt frowned. 'I remember him mentioning some domestic trouble he was worried about. He was pretty vague and obviously anxious. I gave him a few relaxation techniques to help with panic attacks. As he had signed on as a temporary resident, I asked him to see me again in the hope that I might get to know him a little better.'

They were silent for a moment, then Abbie spoke. 'Have you tried talking to Rendale Activity Centre yet?'

The doctor nodded. 'They appear to know even less about the man. He seemed to have kept very much to himself.'

'They've no contact number?' Abbie asked.

'Apparently not.'

Finally deciding there was little more that could be done, Abbie and Matt left the unit. 'Well, that revealed little,' Matt said with a sigh as they arrived at his car and climbed in.

'Perhaps someone who knows him will enquire at the activity centre,' Abbie said, feeling less certain about that than she sounded.

Matt nodded as he reached out to start the car. Then, withdrawing his hand slowly, he sat back in his seat and turned to face her. 'I was wondering if you would like to help me celebrate a house-warming tonight,' he said with a hesitant smile. 'I moved into a new place on Friday night. It's just a small terraced house, but there's a bottle of wine in the fridge that needs opening.'

'You mean, you've left Phil's?' Abbie asked in surprise.

He nodded. 'I felt I'd put on Phil enough. Besides which he has frequent company these days.'

It was a moment or two before Abbie understood. 'You mean Joely?'

He nodded. 'So, as I'm to be in Rendale a little while, I thought it best to find somewhere close to the surgery.'

'In that case,' she said hesitantly, lifting her shoulders in a shrug, 'I'd like to help you celebrate your new home.'

'You'll have to forgive the mess,' he said as he started the car and, glancing in his driving mirror, reversed out of the parking space. 'I haven't got myself sorted out yet. I've only been in a couple of days.'

'Where is it?' Abbie asked curiously.

'A few doors from Jasper, as it happens.' He gave her a crooked smile. 'I've a few things in the fridge, nothing special, though. Do you want me to stop for something?'

She shook her head, commenting that whatever he had to offer was fine. The butterflies inside her stomach were leaving little room for an appetite.

*   *   *

Jasper's was a large house set back behind a low row of shrubs. There was no sign of life, though, and as they passed neither of them commented.

It was a beautiful evening when they stepped out of the car. The terraced house still had a To Let sign in the hedge and Matt grinned as he unlocked the front door. 'Welcome,' he said as she moved past him and into the hallway. 'Straight ahead for the kitchen.'

She pushed open a pine door and smiled at the small, cosy kitchen. 'It's lovely, Matt.'

'You haven't seen the rest of it, but shall we eat first?'

She nodded, realising she was hungry. 'All right. What have you got?'

He opened the fridge and Abbie stared inside, pleasantly surprised at the well-stocked shelves. In the end they opted for omelette, salad and a bottle of wine. Abbie prepared the salad while Matt cooked the omelette. They sat at the kitchen table to eat ravenously, though they drank little.

When the meal was over they washed up, put away the dishes and recorked the bottle of wine. Then he showed her the back garden, overgrown and pungent with the flowers that had miraculously survived in their neglected beds.

'It's a pity to have let the garden run down,' Abbie said quietly. 'It's so pretty.'

Matt stretched beside her. 'At least it's private. The fence is strong and there's a deckchair in the shed. That's enough for me.'

She turned to face him, the evening drawing in around them, her heart quickening as she looked up at him. 'Have you ever thought about settling down?' she asked. 'I mean, in Australia?'

He shrugged, leaning back against the well-worn timber of the shed. 'Once there was someone, but the practicality of the thing was less appealing than the idea.'

'You lived together?'

He nodded. 'For a while. Until she decided the commitments of a doctor's life didn't meet her expectations. And, to be fair, she had a life of her own.'

'Doing what?' Abbie asked curiously.

'She was a PA for an oil executive.' His smile was ironic. 'She's married now, jet-setting from one continent to another all in the name of oil. Lisa wasn't a home-maker. At least, not my kind of home. Kids and nappies weren't part of her career strategy.'

'You wanted a family?' she asked in surprise. 'And not Lisa?'

He nodded. 'I did then. My timing was wrong, I guess.' He smiled, reaching out to draw her into his arms. 'However, that was a long time ago. But I know what I want right at this moment,' he said huskily. 'The question is, do you?'

For a while she gazed up at him, the question in his eyes clear, and a warm thrill went through her as she nodded. His lips covered hers and almost as though the conclusion to the day were inevitable, he wound his fingers into her hers and led her upstairs as the last of the evening light faded around them.

They undressed where they stood, Matt staring at her with hungry eyes as naked, they embraced, his arms holding her in a warmth she had never known before. Lips touched briefly then parted. He drew her to the bed and they lay for a while, savouring what was before them as slowly his kisses awoke in her an excitement that she could barely contain.

Their love-making was tender, Matt careful as he made love to her to wait for her response. Arousing in her all the needs that had been for so long neglected, her eagerness was such that Abbie would never have once considered it relevant to her own powers of sexuality. But Matt had woken something inside her. It was awesome and a little frightening. His lips moved over hers, his hands caressing her body, drawing soft groans from her throat, until she could hold herself back no longer.

'Abbie…you're beautiful,' he whispered, as the moment came and he gave her no opportunity to answer as his body tautened and shuddered above her. They lay together afterwards, her body replete with satisfaction. Love-making had never been like this with Sean, she realised as she lay contentedly in Matt's arms. Perhaps it had been because they had known each other for so long or perhaps, more truthfully, she had always feared that real passion had never been part of their relationship.

As her thoughts hovered on the past, Matt moved beside her. His arms closed around her again and one hand slid the length of her spine. She could feel his arousal and her heart pounded as desire filled her again and his kisses sparked the passion that had slept within her for so long until tonight.

In the morning Abbie awoke in the unfamiliar surroundings of the tiny cottage bedroom. One dormer window gave out to the dusky sky and a dazzling array of stars. The room was barely light, the walls reflecting the shadows of the swaying trees outside. Abbie stretched lazily in the surprisingly comfortable double bed, its sheets disordered by their night of love-making.

She felt the warm, hard lines of Matt's body next to her and thought that she could stay here for hours, content to lie in his arms.

He moved then, drawing her against him, his hand smoothing across her hips to gently cup her breasts. Her hands slid around his neck and she moved her fingers into his hair, loving the familiar sensation of his body beside her. Resigning herself to the fact that they had some while ahead of them before rising, she lifted her face to his kiss.

*   *   *

'If I promise to cook you breakfast,' Abbie said as dawn broke properly and they lay in each other's arms, 'could I persuade you into strolling down the road for some newspapers? We could sit in the garden afterwards and eat.'

'I think I can oblige.' He kissed her softly then leaned on his elbow to gaze into her eyes. 'Abbie, about us…?'

She smiled as she looked up at him. 'Are you asking me if I think we should go on seeing one another?'

He stroked her hair away from her face and nodded. 'Yes, I suppose I am.'

She hesitated as she gazed at the golden brown skin and dark eyes that made her heart beat faster. Tracing a path with his index finger over the curve of her neck, he lifted his eyes and added, 'I want to see more of you, but you may feel differently. And I don't want you to feel you're committed for the next six months.' He hesitated then shrugged.

She lifted an eyebrow. 'So what is it that you're suggesting?

'That we take this as it comes,' he said quietly. 'What we have feels rather special to me.' He paused, looking at her levelly. 'But as soon as you feel you need breathing space, I'd like you to say so. It won't make any difference to our working relationship and that's a promise.'

She understood what he meant. And she was grateful to him for saying what he had. She lay back against the pillow and wondered what it would be like to have a lover after all these years. At the moment her body felt marvellous, her ego flattered. What more could she ask of life for the moment?

He brought her closer, his arms tightening around her as he bent to whisper, 'Well, I'm willing to go along with whatever you say, but right now there is just one more thing…'

Abbie arched her eyebrows as he tugged the sheet up

over their heads, effectively postponing their plans for breakfast.

Serena Kay gave birth to a healthy baby girl on the first day of May. Graham phoned Abbie at the surgery just as she was concluding the practice meeting with Matt, Frank, the receptionists, Jill Nials the secretary, practice nurse Betty Trowbridge and district nurse Jackie Dunn.

Their agenda had covered the loss of Bonnie to the staff, the addition of Matt's TR surgeries and the somewhat vexed question of a children's clinic.

Graham's call had come at eight-thirty in the morning, before surgery, when all the staff, after the first half-hour of brainstorming, welcomed the excuse to conclude the meeting.

'Rachel, would you ring back Graham Kay for me and tell him I'll call by the hospital later today?' Abbie asked as the meeting broke up.

Rachel nodded. 'Will do.'

'Matt?' Abbie called as Matt's tall figure hovered on the other side of the room. 'Have you a minute to spare?'

He nodded and followed her into the corridor and along to her room. There, when the door was firmly closed behind them, he bent to kiss her briefly, allowing her to move away as noises came from the corridor.

'How do you think everyone feels about the children's clinic?' he asked, clearing his throat as they smiled at one another as the footsteps passed and they each took a seat.

'I think everyone's in agreement,' she replied, as her thoughts wandered to the few private occasions they had managed to share together since their day at Grassmere. The morning after they had made love he had driven her to the surgery where she had collected her car, then driven back to her own house for breakfast. Her mother, discreet as always, had asked few questions, but Abbie had explained truthfully that she had spent the night at Matt's house.

As she glanced out of the window she wondered what it would be like to be with Matt on a day like this, rowing across Grassmere Lake and stopping for a picnic on a hillside.

'I can count on your support?' Matt's voice broke into her thoughts and she turned to look at him. He was smiling, one eyebrow crooked up.

'That's blackmail,' she said with a frown as he leaned across the desk and nodded, his dark eyes roving her face.

'The point is, is it working?'

'You'll have to persuade Jill to work out suitable times.' She hesitated, trying to ignore the small thrill that went through her as he touched her fingers and drew the pad of his thumb over her palm.

'All right, that seems reasonable.' He sat back, producing a folded sheet of white A4 paper from his shirt pocket. 'I've worked the clinic out—roughly. After school would be best and at the end of the week. An hour on Friday evenings, for instance.'

'I think we have a smokers' clinic then,' Abbie said, going to her desk and running her finger along the timetable sheet, her glance straying once more to the window. The Lakes would be at their most beautiful, the skies their bluest, at this time of year, and she suddenly yearned to see it all on a day like this with Matt.

'No problem,' Matt was saying, unaware of her thoughts. 'If the nurse is here, all the better.'

'It's an idea,' Abbie agreed absently. 'You probably wouldn't finish until late.'

He shrugged. 'I shan't ask the staff to stay on.'

Abbie nodded slowly. 'Well, it's worth a try—'

'I've tentatively booked a clinic for next Friday,' he told her, a rueful smile on his face. 'Janine Gillette, ear infections; Michael Ferguson, learning difficulties; Susan Cox, behavioural problems; and Katey Marsh, dietary problems.'

Abbie sat back and grinned. 'You have been busy.'

'Of course, it might be just the first flush of enthusiasm. I might find myself with nothing to do. But, then, no harm done.'

Abbie could see he was determined to put his ideas into practice but she had to admit she had mixed feelings on the subject. However, right at this moment, her thoughts remained selfishly on something far removed from Matt's clinic.

She dropped the pencil, leaned her elbows on the desk and cupped her chin in her palms. 'I was wondering...' she began, and stopped.

'You haven't been concentrating,' he said with mock disappointment, also leaning forward.

'How did you guess?'

'The glazed look.' He chuckled. 'It's a dead give-away.'

She smiled, lifting her eyebrows. 'I was thinking how nice it would be to take a break. A couple of days somewhere while the weather is like this.'

'I think that's a wonderful idea,' he agreed at once. 'I'm just surprised you feel that way too. When were you thinking of?'

'The last weekend in May or the first in June?' she said. 'We can organise our duties by then.'

His mouth curved in a wry smile. 'How much excitement can a man stand in one day?'

She pulled across her notebook and scribbled on a page. 'Don't forget to make a date in your diary.'

'It's already done,' he said huskily. 'And in the meantime how about supper this evening?'

'I'd love to but I'm on duty,' she sighed.

'So? You have to eat and I've something special for the

oven. Tell you what, we'll behave ourselves and just indulge in wholesome conversation.'

She leaned back in her chair and grimaced. 'I didn't know you had an oven.'

He smirked. 'I will have as soon as I move it back in from the garage. The previous tenants evicted it in order to use that miserable little microwave.'

The telephone rang and Abbie answered it. 'My first patient is here,' she mouthed, and he sighed, rising from the chair to amble across the room to the door.

'See you tonight,' she called as she cupped the telephone against her shoulder. He nodded, giving her a crooked smile as he closed the door.

That evening, after visiting Serena and her little girl, Monica, Abbie shared Matt's evening meal. It provided her with an insight into his character that was surprising for a man who professed he had trouble boiling an egg.

In the newly cleaned oven he cooked them baked trout in a smooth mushroom sauce, followed by his cheat-dish of tinned custard and apple pie. The meal was impressive. She was about so say so when her pager went off.

'It was wonderful while it lasted,' she sighed as she pushed her chair back from the table.

'But duty calls?' He watched her pick up her case, his eyes following her as she moved across the room.

'Arthur Haskins.' She added, 'Stomach upset.'

'Our Arthur of the three cigars a day?' He quirked a doubtful eyebrow. 'Are you coming back to finish the cheese and biscuits?'

'You haven't any,' she said laughingly as she pulled on her sweater. 'Thank you anyway.' She kissed him as he took her in his arms. 'I have to admit the temptation to come back here is enormous.'

'Were you really serious today when you mentioned going away for a few days?' he asked her, frowning.

She nodded. 'Yes. Why not?'

He kissed her again, threatening that the next time they ate dinner it would be without the encumbrance of the small gadget in her blouse pocket.

He saw her off, waving to her from the doorstep of the cottage. But as she drove past Jasper's house her mood changed as stirrings of unease returned to trouble her. Jasper had made an appointment for the following Friday. By then she would almost certainly have received the results of his tests. And she knew in her heart what they would be.

CHAPTER FIVE

ABBIE'S visit to Arthur Haskins was more than surprising. To start with, Arthur, though quite ill with a stomach upset, had abandoned his beloved cigars.

'How long have you not smoked?' Abbie asked as she wrote a prescription for Dioralyte.

'Two weeks,' said Arthur weakly. 'Since my last attack of angina.' He lay in bed, looking very sorry for himself.

'What made you decide to stop smoking?' Abbie gave the prescription to Arthur's wife, Elspeth.

'A story about an Aborigine,' replied Arthur.

Abbie looked up. 'A what?'

'It was a story about this old Aborigine who smoked like a chimney,' said Elspeth. 'One day, he rolled a wild plant in the bush and smoked it. He almost died. Luckily, he recovered in hospital. Except that when he came out of his coma it was six weeks later.'

'He was seventy-two,' added Arthur. 'And he went on to live till he was a hundred and two.'

'That's thirty years,' Elspeth remarked. 'Dr Carrig saw Arthur two weeks ago when he had a nasty angina attack. He asked Arthur to visualise he'd just woken out of a coma. Then he asked him if he would like the chance to live for another thirty years.'

'I'd never thought of it that way,' said Arthur. 'That's why I've decided to give it a go. Mind you, I've had this stomach upset for nearly a week and haven't fancied one.'

'Well, you've had a nasty bout of gastro-enteritis,' Abbie said as she stood up. 'The Dioralyte will replace the fluid and salts lost in acute diarrhoea. You'll begin to feel better soon and start to eat again. It's then that you might feel like your cigar.'

'Tell Dr Carrig I'm still visualising my extra thirty years,' Arthur said. 'That's thirty more dart match finals at the Boar's Head. I can't afford to miss those. We might even get in the top league by then.'

'Him and his darts,' murmured Elspeth as she showed Abbie to the front door. 'Your Dr Carrig certainly knew Arthur's Achilles heel.'

It was a remark that, next day, Abbie repeated to Matt who, as she told him, began to grin.

'I wondered if it might do the job,' he commented as they walked together from the car park to the surgery. Abbie was about to take the two-hour emergency surgery held on Saturday mornings and Matt the house calls.

'You're a dark horse,' she teased. 'You didn't say anything about visiting Arthur and reeling him off stories of poisonous weeds.'

'I didn't know if creative visualisation would work with Arthur,' he told her with a grin. Then, stopping just before they arrived at the front door, he bent closer and whispered, 'Though I have to say it has worked wonders on a personal level.'

They stood for a while, locked into one another's gaze, and then Abbie jumped as someone flattened a palm on a car horn as several children clambered noisily from a car, indicating that their intimate moment was over.

It was on the following Thursday—one day before Jasper's official appointment on Friday—that Abbie found herself driving towards his house. She was answering a request for a house call which Rachel had taken over the phone.

When Abbie arrived at the house and turned into the drive she hesitated. She pulled on the handbrake slowly in order to give herself time to think. She had received the results of Jasper's EMG tests—the measurement of electrical activity in wasting muscle—and a biopsy of tissue that linked with blood tests to give a clear indication of motor neurone disease.

Not looking forward to giving him the news, she took a breath. Then she pulled her case from the back seat and climbed out of the car.

Unusually, the door of the house was open. Abbie cautiously pushed it a little wider. 'Jasper?' She waited but there was no reply. 'Is anyone there?'

She entered the hall with a sense of foreboding, then searched the downstairs rooms. It was an old house, all dark, polished wood and Indian rugs. Abbie identified a smell of camphor and leapt the stairs two at a time.

In one of the large bedrooms upstairs she found Jasper. Her heart plummeted. He lay in his old Victorian double bed, his eyes closed, the aroma of camphor thick in the room. Suddenly he seemed to gulp and began a fit of coughing.

'Jasper, what's happened?' she asked sharply, helping him to sit up. She propped the pillows behind him.

Abbie handed him a glass of water from the bedside cabinet. He gulped back the fluid, then sank against the pillows. 'Had bit of trouble b-breathing,' he wheezed. 'Managed to get downstairs…phone you…leave the door open.'

Abbie gently pushed open his pyjama jacket and placed her stethoscope on his chest. It took her only a few seconds to discover an acute chest infection. 'How long have you been like this?' she asked.

'Not long…a couple of days perhaps. Been using camphor to clear the airways. Usually does the trick.'

'Jasper, why didn't you telephone me?' She had no real need to ask the question—she was in no doubt of the answer.

'Thought it was a cold, that's all. Got a bit wet on one of the tours last week,' he answered weakly.

'It may have started as a cold but you now have an infection. I'm afraid I'm going to have to admit you.'

'No way, girl!' he protested, and began to cough again.

'You need a ventilator and drugs to help clear the congestion,' she said quietly after the coughing fit was over. 'Sorry, Jasper, but I have to insist.' Abbie left him grumbling as she hurried downstairs to the telephone.

Fortunately the hospital could provide a bed and the ambulance arrived quickly. Abbie packed Jasper an overnight bag and promised she would visit him that evening. However, she had still not given him the test results and it weighed on her mind.

Back at the surgery she found Matt in Reception, bending over the appointment book. Her concern for Jasper must have been evident as he looked up and met her eyes.

'Problems?' He drew her to one side, away from the queue.

'I had Jasper's results today,' she explained.

'And it's motor neurone disease?'

'Yes, I'm afraid so. I've just admitted him to Rendale Cottage Hospital with a chest infection. He'd been dosing himself with camphor. It's his infallible remedy which he's used for years, but it wasn't doing him any good at this stage. Somehow he managed to phone in. A few hours more and he would never have been strong enough to climb out of bed.'

Matt's face clouded. 'You haven't had the opportunity to discuss the test results with him?'

'No. I'm afraid I still have to break that news.'

He nodded and said nothing. Then he looked up. 'I'm due to make a visit to the Kays shortly.'

Abbie drew her thoughts back to Graham and Serena Kay. 'Monica is a lovely little girl—no trouble, I hope?'

'I don't think so. A wind problem by all accounts.' He grinned. 'But I thought you might like to come along so I said I would visit during the lunch-hour. We could eat on the way back at the White Hart.'

At that moment Frank Morgan joined them. Abbie broke the news of Jasper.

'I'll look in and see him tonight,' Frank said on a sigh. 'Are you going to visit him, Abbie?'

She nodded. 'Yes, I'll see you there.'

'How are you doing, Matt?' Frank turned his attention to the younger doctor. 'When is this brave new clinic of yours?'

Abbie left them talking and returned to her consulting room. She took a few minutes to sift through the papers on her desk. Reflecting that it would be a welcome distraction to see little Monica Kay again and then relax for half an hour over lunch with Matt, she endeavoured to put Jasper's unhappy plight from her thoughts.

The visit to the Kays, however, did not run as smoothly as she had hoped. Monica was a healthy little girl and was merely suffering from wind. Abbie chatted to Serena while Matt continued to examine Monica.

But while Serena made tea, Matt gestured to the baby's right leg. 'Monica's heel turns inward…here.' He gestured to the small foot and drew his thumb and forefinger over the area.

'Yes, it does,' Abbie agreed.

'This looks like a mild form of talipes to me.'

'Club-foot?' Abbie sighed as she made a closer inspection of Monica's heel. 'The hospital didn't spot it but, then, sometimes it isn't visible immediately. Do you think it will need orthopaedic splinting?'

Matt paused. 'I think we might be able to avoid that encumbrance. We need to stretch the foot by gentle movements and exercise. Make the tightened tendon more flexible.'

'Serena is going to be upset,' Abbie said.

'I'll ask her to come into clinic,' Matt decided, rubbing his chin. 'I'll set up a regime of exercises which she can perform herself. That way she will feel she is actively involved in correcting the problem.' He looked up and smiled as Serena came into the room with a tray of tea.

But Serena took the news badly and it was some time before Matt and Abbie left the house.

'Hopefully, Serena will turn up for clinic,' Matt observed as he pushed a sandwich disinterestedly around his plate at the White Hart. 'She didn't seem too enthusiastic.'

'She's upset,' Abbie agreed.

They were silent for a while then, pushing his plate away from him, he glanced at his watch and sighed. 'One forty-five. Much as I'd like to sit here for the afternoon, there's work to do.'

Abbie finished her lemonade and they left. At the entrance he looked back and held out his hand. She took it, her heart giving a little flip at its warm reassurance.

They had walked no more than a few feet before they saw Joely and Phil. Joely explained that she had an afternoon off work and they were lunching out, before collecting Michele from school.

'Enjoy your lunch,' Abbie said.

'Catch up with you soon,' Joely called, grinning.

Matt smiled as they climbed into the Citroën. 'I think we can take it that your sister and Phil are seeing quite a bit of one another.'

Abbie nodded. 'Which is probably what they are saying about us right now.'

During her visit to the hospital that evening Abbie went to see Dave Carter. He was now out of danger and due to be transferred from the ICU to a ward the following day.

They were soon joined by a young woman who sat quietly in a chair at his bedside. Abbie guessed she was his girlfriend, though no introductions were made. Explaining that she must leave in order to visit another patient, Abbie bade them both goodbye.

But in the corridor outside the girl hurried after her. She introduced herself formally as Marion Foster.

'I'm Dave's girlfriend,' she explained. 'Do you think he will be all right, Dr Ashby? I think this is all my fault.'

Abbie asked her why she thought that.

'Dave is divorced and is older than me by eleven years. My parents object and there have been terrible family rows. My parents object to us seeing one another because, amongst other things, he hasn't got a proper job. They say working as a sports instructor is just a way of meeting girls. I think the worry of it all causes his panic attacks.'

'Have you talked to Dave about it?' Abbie asked.

'I've tried, but he just says he thinks we should stop seeing each other.'

'When Dave is feeling better,' Abbie suggested on impulse, 'come into the surgery with him and we'll talk. In the meantime, try not to worry.'

The young woman smiled. 'Thanks a lot, Dr Ashby. I'll tell Dave.'

A few minutes later Abbie sat next to Frank Morgan at Jasper's bedside and noted that his breathing, assisted by a hospital ventilator, was easier. Jasper himself brought up the subject of the tests and Abbie answered as honestly as she could.

'I thought as much,' Jasper said, and smiled. 'It's better to know, strangely enough.'

'There's a lot we can do,' said Frank supportively.

'And a lot I don't want done,' commented Jasper wryly.

Abbie saw that he was tired and stayed only a few minutes longer, leaving Frank to keep vigil.

Exhaustion claimed her when she arrived home. She ran a bath and soaked in it until Joely rang and she was forced from its silky depths. Wrapped in a towel, she sat on the edge and listened to her sister. After school that day Michele had developed a temperature.

'It never rains but it pours,' commented Bonnie Burchfield that evening as she studied her daughter's pre-occupied face. They sat together in the conservatory, enjoying a supper of salad, balanced on their knees. A tray of tea stood on the rattan table beside them and the sun flooded in through the open patio doors.

'I should really visit Michele,' Abbie sighed. 'She's prone to tonsillitis and this may be the start.'

'Joely said it was just a temperature, darling. It's probably nothing more than a cold.' Bonnie added quietly, 'Do I gather you've had a difficult day?'

Abbie told her mother about Jasper.

'Poor Jasper,' murmured Bonnie. 'All on his own in that huge house. I suppose, as it was his parents' and he's never married, it never occurred to him to buy somewhere more manageable. Will he be able to look after himself when he comes home?'

'He will certainly need help at some point, both with domestic chores and from our nursing team.'

'And Jasper will hate that. He's so independent.'

They sat in silence for a while, then Bonnie told her daughter of the events of her own day.

'How's Don?' Abbie asked.

'He's enjoying the business course as much as I am,' her mother replied. 'Stuck in an office for years, he's never been able to meet many people. That's the exciting part for us both. It's a whole new world.'

'I'm glad you found someone to enjoy the course with,' Abbie said and smiled.

'Don's a widower,' Bonnie went on. 'He wanted something to occupy his mind after his wife died two years ago.' She blushed and looked at Abbie under her lashes. It wasn't surprising, Abbie reflected, that her mother had met someone, only that she, Abbie, had not been prepared for it. Her mother had made no mention of marrying again, but Don seemed to be an important part of her life now.

As far as her own future was concerned, there would come a time when Matt would return to Australia and life would return to its normal pattern…

Her mother frowned, catching the far-away expression in her daughter's eyes. 'Is there something troubling you, Abbie?'

Abbie looked at her mother and, bringing herself back from her thoughts of Matt, smiled. 'No… I was just thinking how wonderful you're looking these days.'

'Oh, Abbie.' Bonnie smiled. 'You can fool some of the people some of the time, but you can't fool your mother at all.'

Her mother's reaction caught Abbie unawares and for a moment she was silent.

Bonnie added slowly, 'It's Matt, isn't it? You've grown very fond of him.'

Abbie knew there was no point in denying it and she nodded. 'Yes, I have.'

'Does he feel the same way about you?'

Abbie looked at her mother. 'If you mean is there anything that can come of it,' Abbie replied, 'then the answer is no. He's returning to Australia in the autumn. We both knew that from the beginning and were under no illusions as to the outcome.'

The silence deepened until Bonnie changed the topic of conversation. 'Don and I are going to the theatre on

Saturday,' she said after a moment's thought. 'I haven't anything really appropriate to wear. I wondered if you would help me choose something on Saturday morning. Or are you in surgery?'

'No, Frank is on duty.' Abbie smiled. 'Saturday morning will be fine, Mum,' she agreed, greatly relieved that her mother had tactfully changed the painful subject of Matt's departure to a happier one.

Matt's first clinic turned out to be a resounding success. Mrs Gillette, about to pass Abbie in the hall, stopped to comment.

'Dr Carrig is so understanding,' she trilled. 'We discussed Janine's recurrent ear infections and narrowed down some causes. For instance, all the swimming she does. He's teaching Janine a technique that the Olympic swimmers use. They equalise the pressure across the eardrum—that's the secret. I'm really impressed.'

Abbie listened, wondering if Mrs Gillette's hotly flushed face was entirely due to Matt's suggestions on Olympic techniques. However, Janine seemed satisfied, too, as she puffed out her cheeks and swallowed loudly in eager demonstration of the exercise.

Not to be outdone, Mrs Marsh and Katey followed hard on the heels of Mrs Gillette and Janine. Katey was overweight for a nine-year-old, but Matt, according to Mrs Marsh, had simply recommended some reading material.

After the clinic Abbie joined Matt in the staffroom. Matt poured them coffee and sank into the comfortable chair beside her.

'This is an unexpected treat, to find you still here,' he said as he crossed his long legs and stirred his coffee thoughtfully.

'I'm intrigued,' she confessed.

'With me, I hope.' He chuckled. 'Is it the aftershave or the haircut?'

His hair had grown thick and rather wild again and looked disarmingly sexy as it fell across his forehead. 'It's neither, although I like both.' She laughed. 'Actually, it's the feedback I had from your clinic patients. Everyone was delighted.'

'Really?' He frowned. 'I was busy enough. Everyone turned up on time. Even Serena and Monica. But no one said very much.'

It was characteristic of him to keep his comments low key. She found herself pursuing the subject with real curiosity. 'Your suggestion to Katey Marsh—to read a book?' she prompted.

He smiled. 'Ah, yes—*What Katey Does in the Kitchen*.'

'I don't think I know it,' Abbie murmured.

He hesitated. 'Well, we can't put kids on diets but we can help them to see the sense of avoiding junk food. *What Katey Did in the Kitchen* is a brilliant story about a little girl who wins a cookery competition at school. Her granny gives her a really old recipe which turns out to be a hit with the class. The book's filled with jokes and good wholesome food that kids can help their mothers prepare.'

'Don't tell me you are a secret Enid Blyton reader still!' she teased.

He laughed again, lifting his eyebrows. 'No, this was a book my sister read years ago when she was overweight.'

'Your sister?' Abbie looked surprised. 'I know you have a brother, Matt. I didn't realise you also had a sister.'

He looked down at the rim of his cup and drew a finger slowly over the gold-rimmed edge. 'Her name was Frances. She was fifteen when she died. It was one of the reasons we emigrated. Dad thought it was probably best to get away and make a fresh start.'

'Oh, Matt. How tragic.'

'It was meningitis. A cluster at Fran's school. The other girls recovered but Fran was unlucky.'

Abbie was silent, then after a while she said, 'I'm sure Katey will love the book. Is it still available in the shops?'

He paused. 'I'm not sure, but I've a copy with me. Oddly enough I happened to find one in a London bookstore. It has a real message for kids. She's welcome to borrow it until I go back to Adelaide.'

The mention of his return to Adelaide reminded Abbie that she was beginning to take for granted the happiness she had found with Matt and until her mother had spoken to her on the subject she had managed to put it to the back of her mind. There was no doubt that Matt would return to his home and career in Australia—it was a fact she was forced to accept. As she had explained to her mother, there was no commitment between them—she had embarked upon their affair in full knowledge of the circumstances.

Nevertheless, here in the softness of the beautiful May evening outside, with the blue sky overhead shimmering with pale stars, the Cumbrian horizon awash with pink and golden light, as they exchanged confidences and shared thoughts, she could pretend that time was their own and her happiness might go on for ever.

On Saturday Kate drove her mother to the town centre and helped her choose a smart new suit for her date that evening. Undoubtedly her mother was both nervous and excited, emotions which Abbie was not unfamiliar with herself.

They parted company after a light lunch, her mother going on to an appointment at the hairdresser's and Abbie to collect Michele for her dancing class. Abbie arrived at the cottage to discover that Michele had now developed the beginnings of a sore throat. Not wanting to give her antibiotics before it was necessary, Abbie advised Joely to keep Michele in bed for the day.

'Did you enjoy your lunch with Matt?' Joely asked as they sipped coffee together at the kitchen bar afterwards.

'Mmm,' Abbie answered. 'How about you and Phil?'

'Mmm.' Joely murmured in the same tone. 'Just sandwiches and shandy.'

They both looked at one another and then laughed, neither of them about to question the other.

'Do you know Mum has a date tonight?' Joely said after a while.

Abbie grinned. 'Yes. Did she tell you?'

Joely nodded. 'When I rang her about Michele.' Standing up to refresh their coffee-mugs, Joely said what Abbie was thinking. 'It's time Mum started enjoying herself. I really hope it works out for them.'

Abbie nodded. 'Me, too.' It seemed, she reflected as she watched her sister move about the kitchen, that life had changed for all three women in the family and that, whatever might happen in the future, the coming summer was due to hold happiness for each of them.

By the time Abbie got home, Bonnie had changed into her elegant black suit and ivory cream blouse. Much to Abbie's surprise, she had also bought an entirely new perfume, the scent of which filled the top floor of the house. The hairdresser had shaped her fair hair around her face, making her look much younger.

'I'm nervous,' Bonnie admitted as she stood waiting in the hall for Don to arrive. 'Do I look all right in this suit? Is it too sophisticated?'

'You look wonderful,' Abbie said with an admiring smile. 'Don's going to be very impressed.'

'Thank you, darling.' Her mother paused. 'I just wish that you—'

A car horn sounded and, without finishing her sentence, Bonnie leaned forward and kissed her daughter, then made a hurried exit for her date.

Reflecting that Bonnie had almost certainly been on the point of saying something about Matt, Abbie was grateful that Don had arrived and the moment had passed. Her mother meant well, but going over the same ground—Matt's departure—would achieve nothing except a repeated sense of dismay.

Abbie watched the car disappear and closed the front door. She turned her thoughts to practical matters, wondering if she should cook a meal or merely make herself a snack. She was on call that evening and opted for a sandwich. Moments after she had eaten it, her pager went off.

The call was to a troubled asthma patient, a boy of fourteen. Using a nebuliser to assist the teenager's breathing, she returned home, only to go out again at ten o'clock to a baby with what turned out to be teething trouble.

At just after midnight she returned home in time to meet her mother who was standing on the doorstep. A car parked on the opposite side of the road pulled away and flashed its lights. Bonnie waved back. 'That was Don,' she said as Abbie pushed her own key in the lock.

'Did you enjoy the theatre?' Abbie thought her mother looked flushed and elated.

'Wonderful!' Bonnie exclaimed, eager to talk about her evening. 'The play was a comedy of errors and had a marvellous cast of quite well-known actors. I haven't laughed so much in years.' She glanced quickly in the hall mirror, patting her hot cheeks. 'Oh, goodness, whatever do I look like?'

'You look lovely, Mum,' Abbie said quietly. 'You know you do. And I'm sure Don thought so, too.'

Her mother turned and smiled, taking a deep breath.

'Yes, he did say so. I would have liked you to meet him but it was a bit late…'

'You should have asked him in for coffee.' Abbie took off her coat and hung it on the hallstand.

'Yes, I will next time.' Her mother looked flustered. 'On our way to the theatre we called in to see how Michele was, and Phil happened to be there.'

Abbie smiled. 'I'm not surprised. Phil and Joely seem to be an item these days.'

'He's very nice,' Bonnie commented. 'And seems to get on well with Michele.'

Avoiding her mother's curious glance, Abbie said, 'So do I take it you introduced Don?'

They both laughed as Bonnie flushed. 'Oh, darling, I hope you'll like him, too.'

Abbie hugged her mother. 'I know I will, Mum. Now, I think we'd both better try to get some sleep.'

But instead of going to bed, Abbie sat on the window-seat in her bedroom and looked out over the garden. A full moon lit up the row of conifers that her father had planted many years ago and which Sean had trimmed, balancing on the top of a long ladder.

Life had changed after their deaths and she had never considered the possibility of falling in love again, certain that Sean had been the one love of her life. But that had changed now. Abbie stirred restlessly as her body responded to the thought of Matt's love-making and the times she had spent in his arms.

Matt, whose nature was so entirely different to Sean's, and yet she had loved Sean, hadn't she? In a different way, yes, she answered herself, attempting to be truthful. He had been her friend and partner and they had shared many years together, but their life had remained unfulfilled without children.

Admitting the fact now was easier. It was because she

had found the truth so hard to accept that she had been afraid to analyse her feelings. Her relationship with Matt had caused her to discover that she had repressed her true feelings, knowing that Sean had been content with his life and career.

With a sigh she dragged herself away from the window and set the alarm for the morning. Even if there were no more calls during the night, she would probably not sleep deeply. Too much had gone on during the day to stimulate her brain.

The only cure would be Matt. And he, sadly, was not there to give it.

It was the last weekend in May which Abbie had selected for her break with Matt. Jill Nials had arranged for Bob Wesley in Hobcraig to cover the duty calls, and much to Abbie's surprise there were no last-minute problems to hinder their teatime departure.

Matt's Friday clinic finished slightly earlier than usual, allowing them to leave the practice at five and drive to Keswick and to their room at the lakeside hotel which Matt had pre-booked.

Leaving Rendale behind, the road wound ahead, a shimmering ribbon of light, the sun tracing a path through the landscape with a golden finger. On either side the hills and fells grew misty with heat. Some of the peaks remained hidden from view by low cloud, only a glint of high white snow sparkling from a gap in the billowy vapour.

'Where would you like to eat?' Matt asked, glancing at his watch. 'We might be in time to catch the hotel restaurant before it closes or we could eat somewhere else.'

'There's a little restaurant at Gowbarrow Fell,' Abbie replied thoughtfully. 'I haven't been there for years, but they used to serve some wonderful Lakeland dishes.'

'Then that's where we're headed,' said Matt, flashing her a smile that made her heart quicken.

'I can't help feeling as though I'm truanting,' Abbie giggled. 'It's so wonderful to be away.'

'And we won't talk shop,' Matt decided firmly.

'Absolutely not,' she agreed.

There was a pause as Abbie arched her eyebrows. 'Could I just ask about *What Katey Did in the Kitchen*?'

Matt threw back his dark head and chuckled. 'That pact didn't last long.'

'I promise, just the one question,' Abbie begged.

'Just the one,' he agreed. 'As it's Katey. Well, Mrs Marsh is reading the book with her. It's a long shot really, but it might plant a seed or two of otherwise untapped thought.'

'One satisfied customer, by the sound of it,' Abbie remarked wryly.

'We aim to please.' Matt glanced at her, his dark eyes twinkling. 'And now I'm hoping for another.'

'Who?' asked Abbie innocently.

'Oh, just someone,' he murmured cryptically. He looked back at the road, a smile crossing his face. 'Now you had better give me the directions to Gowbarrow Fell before I lose us completely and we wind up sleeping in the car at the side of the road.'

Abbie laughed softly, her cheeks flushed with excitement. She was tempted to tell him that as long as she was with him it didn't matter where they were heading because it was wonderful just to be with him and to feel so young again.

But she didn't want to reveal just how happy she was. She didn't want to tempt providence. She could hardly believe that tonight she would go to sleep lying in his arms and for the next two deliriously irresponsible mornings she would wake up to find him lying beside her.

CHAPTER SIX

THE tiny restaurant at Gowbarrow Fell served a delicious meal of hot carrot and coriander soup, Cumbrian pie and cheesecake topped with fresh local cream. They sat in a cosy booth lit by candles and it was late in the evening by the time they finished their meal and arrived in Keswick. The porter at the lakeside hotel showed them to their room and Abbie gasped as she saw the view, a myriad of coloured lights sparkling across the water on the opposite shore and reflected on its inky surface.

Matt slid his arms around her waist and whispered in her hair. 'We're all alone—do you realise that? No man or beast to disturb us.'

'It's so beautiful, Matt,' she sighed, leaning her head back against his shoulder. 'How did you manage to choose such a lovely room?'

'I'm telepathic, remember?' He nestled his cheek against her. 'I knew it had be the most romantic room in the hotel.'

'No.' she laughed softly. 'I'm serious.'

'And so am I.' He turned her slowly towards him and there over his shoulder she saw a four-poster bed decorated in white frills and a voluptuous cream silk quilt. On a circular glass table stood a huge display of flowers and next to it a silver ice bucket containing the slender green neck of a champagne bottle.

'Oh, Matt…what have you done?' She could hardly believe her eyes.

'Well, I think we deserve it, don't you?'

She swallowed. 'You're spoiling me.'

'You deserve to be spoiled,' he whispered and lifting her

chin, he gazed into her eyes, his own dark brown ones hungry with desire. 'Now, are you going to pop the cork or shall I?'

It was, as it happened, an unnecessary question. Their desire overtook them and he made love to her immediately, both the unpacking and champagne abandoned as they took each other's bodies with a reckless desperation.

Later, as she lay in his arms, they sipped the bubbling liquid until in the early hours they finally fell asleep.

It was the unfamiliar noise on the lake that woke her— a flight of wildfowl. She turned and gazed into the face on the pillow beside her. Long, black lashes lay on his cheeks, his strong features relaxed in sleep. For a moment she thought how young he looked and her heart gave a little lurch. The age difference had never seemed to bother him so why should she start to worry about it now? As though he was reading her thoughts in his sleep, he opened his eyes.

'Hmm, that's nice,' he whispered, sleepily pulling her towards him. 'You weren't thinking of getting up, I hope.'

'It's only just light,' she murmured, her words broken by his kisses.

'That's good.' He smoothed her hair from her face and looked into her eyes. 'Now come here, and let me say a proper good morning.'

By nine, a heat haze had begun to spread over the water, floating across the sparkling surface like a magic carpet. Sounds of early morning activity came from the car park and Abbie, fully dressed in shorts and T-shirt, saw a young couple piling hiking boots and backpacks into the rear of their camper.

'Early birds?' Matt came to stand behind her, sliding his arms around her waist as he had last night.

'I think they arrived about the same time as us,' Abbie murmured, remembering smiling at the girl in the foyer.

At that moment the young man leaned across and kissed the girl, breaking away as another guest walked past.

Abbie sighed as she leaned against Matt's chest. 'They look so absorbed in one another. Do you think they are leaving?'

'Looking for a little peace and quiet, I should think,' commented Matt ruefully. He took her hand and turned her to face him. 'Now, let's concentrate on us. What shall we do first?'

'There's a heat haze already...'

'We could sail instead of climbing.'

'You make the decision.' She giggled, feeling almost light-headed with happiness. 'There's so much we can do, I can't decide.'

'Let's settle for a stroll by the lake and a sail after lunch if we feel like it. Or even a row across to that little island. It looks as though it's calling out to be discovered.'

Abbie threaded her arms around his neck. 'Whatever you suggest, Dr Carrig,' she whispered. 'I'm in your hands completely.'

'And that,' he muttered with a grin, 'is precisely where I intend to keep you for the next twenty-four hours.'

In the end they left the car at the hotel and walked into Keswick. On their way they passed the young couple they had seen earlier, heading in the opposite direction in their camper. Abbie smiled at the girl in the passenger seat and Matt nodded to the driver. The vehicle's lights flashed in return.

A few minutes later they turned into a narrow lane that led down to the shore of the lake and made their way around the perimeter. Finally they came to the boating office. Choosing a rowing boat, Matt rowed them across to the tiny island they had seen from their bedroom window.

'I've heard of island-hopping,' Abbie said laughingly as they landed, pulled up the boat and clambered up the grassy bank, 'but this is ridiculous.'

'Not at all,' Matt said as he took her hand and led her into the shady copse. 'Now I really have got you all to myself.'

'And if I screamed no one would hear me?' Abbie teased as he draped a blanket he had brought with him over the mossy grass.

'Do you want to scream?' He lay down and crooked his little finger. 'Or would you prefer to lie down and quietly resign yourself to my care?'

Abbie sank to her knees, hoping that no one else had decided to start the day with an adventure to the island. But if they had, she really didn't care. They would, no doubt, see the boat and guess that somewhere in this small oasis two lovers had already made the island their own.

The evening was sultry and overcast. They dined at the hotel and afterwards listened to the music of the jazz quartet that played in the cocktail bar. Before retiring, they walked beside the lake and kissed under a starlit sky as the water lapped at their feet. Matt whispered, 'Happy?'

She nodded. 'And you?'

'Words fail me,' he murmured as he ran his fingers through her hair, 'but actions don't.' With that he took her in his arms and kissed her and the world seemed to shake under her feet. His hands smoothed over her back, his fingertips tracing a tingling path down her spine. Her breath caught in her throat as she arched against him and a soft cry escaped her lips.

For a few more seconds they stood by the lake, locked in their own little world, until finally Matt slipped his hand around hers and led her back to the hotel.

*   *   *

The following day's break in the weather came with an early fall of rain before breakfast. Dressed in jeans and sweatshirt, Abbie looked out of their bedroom window. Low, bruised-looking clouds hung in the sky and, though it was warm, there was an atmosphere of change in the air.

However, after breakfast they decided to go ahead, choosing a gentle climb up to Skiddrigg Hause, which was relatively accessible. But soon the rain began in earnest and halfway up Skiddrigg heavy sheets of it swept across the countryside.

'Let's take cover,' Matt shouted, and they ran under a thicket of trees, pulling on wet gear over their jeans and T-shirts. 'Better make our way down again,' Matt suggested, helping Abbie back on with her rucksack. 'Looks like the rain's in for the duration.'

They sheltered for a few minutes more then attempted the descent. The deluge turned their path into a moving slide of mud and leaves and halfway down they took shelter again.

As they picked their way carefully, lightning forked across the sky. By the time they arrived at the bottom of Skiddrigg even their protective clothing had failed to keep out the elements.

Drenched and breathless they reached the hotel, only to be met by a commotion at Reception. Two policemen were talking to the manager and several guests.

'Trouble?' Matt asked as they went over.

'Our friends are missing,' said a young man dressed in hiker's clothes. 'Anita and James Harvill. They had a room booked here for Friday night. They drove a big blue and white camper.'

Abbie nodded. 'Yes, we saw them leave.'

'When?' asked the policeman.

'Yesterday morning,' said Abbie, frowning.

'But the last we saw of them,' Matt explained. 'was

when they passed us on the main road going out of Keswick.'

'We left them last night camped in their tent at the foot of Mickelsdale Fell,' said the young man. 'It was a bit of a joke really. They said they wanted to sleep under the stars.'

'Did you find the tent this morning?' the policeman asked.

'No. We assume they made the climb.'

'But it's treacherous up there in bad weather,' commented the hotel manager. 'Didn't they know?'

'They've never done anything like this before,' explained the Harvills' friend. 'It was the whole point of the weekend. They must have thought we'd changed our minds because of the storm, and decided to go it alone.'

Matt frowned. 'Is there a search team going out?'

The policeman nodded. 'While there's daylight, yes. We have a helicopter going over the area, too.'

'If we can help?' Abbie suggested. 'We're both doctors.'

Half an hour later, having changed into dry protective clothing, Abbie and Matt found themselves ascending the rugged terrain of Mickelsdale Fell with four members of the Lakeland Rescue Unit. It was a densely wooded area, and although the professionals knew their way the drenched ground delayed what might have been a straightforward ascent.

By seven the light was fading. The six members of the search team were in radio contact with another group and a helicopter, but by eight o'clock Abbie realised things looked grim.

Darkness fell and they had almost given up hope when Abbie spotted a brightly coloured object flapping in a tree.

It was a crumpled yellow cagoule. A few metres past this they found an empty water container half-covered in mud and leaves. With renewed enthusiasm they continued searching, assisted by the powerful beam of the helicopter.

'Here!' Greg, the team leader, shone his torch on the ground. 'Looks like a rucksack.'

'And here!' called Matt.

Abbie found herself hurrying towards a wavering light. A small green tent stood amidst a clump of trees. The wind and rain had taken its toll. The canvas sagged in the middle and some of the guy ropes had broken.

Greg was the first there and pushed back the flaps. Matt and Abbie followed his beam of light as they all peered in the tent.

'Thank God you've come. Anita's hurt,' gasped the young man who crouched beside his wife on the ground.

Matt crawled across to the young woman who lay flat on her back, moaning softly. 'What happened?' he asked quietly as he began to check her airway, breathing and circulation.

'She fell down a kind of ravine,' James Harville explained weakly. 'She hurt her head and knocked herself out. Somehow I managed to get her back here. It took me ages because I did something to…' His face creased in pain as he tried to straighten his arm.

Abbie shuffled into the confined space. 'Was that very long ago?' she asked, supporting his arm.

'Some time today I think. I've lost all track of time. In the storm Anita slipped and I tried to catch her but the ground gave way beneath our feet. My whole shoulder seemed to lock.'

'It looks as though you've dislocated it,' Abbie agreed as she helped him to remove his coat. 'At the moment there's no muscle spasm so it might be possible to put it back. We need to find a fairly flat surface to do that.'

'There are some rocks outside,' Greg said, having heard

the conversation as he waited at the tent opening. 'Some quite flat ones that might do.'

Abbie backed out of the tent, leaving Matt to tend to Anita, and watched two of the rescue team train torches onto the rocks. The injured man painfully edged himself from the tent. 'Give it a try, Doctor, will you?' he asked weakly. 'I'm not much use to anyone like this.'

With the help of the other men, Abbie helped James stumble across to the rocks. She chose the flattest surface and demonstrated the position she wanted him to take. 'As I support your arm, I want you to roll face down to the stone,' she explained. 'I'll be as gentle as I can.'

The extent of his discomfort was apparent as he tried to follow her instructions. A squall of wind and rain did not help matters and Abbie hesitated as he let out an agonised groan, but on the second attempt Abbie was successful in realigning the dislocated shoulder.

'Oh,' gasped her patient as she helped him into a sitting position.

'You'll be sore,' Abbie explained as he recovered his breath, 'but I don't think you're any the worse for wear. How do you feel?'

He nodded, holding his arm. 'OK, thanks, Doctor. I must get back to Anita. She will be all right, won't she?'

'Stay where you are for a moment,' Abbie instructed. 'I'll find out how your wife is.' Leaving him with one of the team, she returned to the tent and found Matt, dressing Anita's head wound with a roller bandage.

'The cut's quite deep and will need suturing,' he explained. 'I'm concerned about the concussion and the shock. She's also extremely cold. We need to get her to hospital as soon as possible. How is her husband?'

'The shoulder went back in, fortunately.' Abbie smiled as he reached out to squeeze her hand. 'Other than that, very worried about his wife.'

'All set, Doc?' Greg crawled in behind them. 'If we can move her, we'll find somewhere the 'copter can land.'

Matt nodded and they soon had the young woman wrapped in a thermal blanket, strapped securely to a stretcher. As soon as they reached clear ground, they hoisted a windsock as a guide for the crew of the helicopter. Five minutes later the helicopter landed gently, sending out a gust of wet leaves.

Abbie and Matt travelled back with their patients and despite the grumbling of the fading storm the helicopter pilot landed them safely in the grounds of the hospital.

'Did we say we weren't going to talk shop this weekend?' Matt grinned as they relinquished their patients to the care of the A and E staff.

'No doubt we tempted fate,' sighed Abbie, shivering in her damp clothes.

Matt pulled her against him in a powerful hug. 'Come on, let's find some nourishment and warm you up. Hot tea and something to eat, then we'll see about cadging a lift to the hotel.'

'I'll drive you,' Greg told them as he, too, joined them at the drinks dispenser. 'Or come home with me and I'll feed you some bacon and eggs.'

'We have to leave pretty early,' Matt declined gracefully. 'We probably ought to get our heads down for a few hours. But thanks all the same. I'll just go back to A and E and check with the duty doctor to see how the Harvills are.'

Abbie remained with Greg until Matt returned. 'The Harvills are being transferred to wards as we speak,' he told them. 'I don't think there's much more we can do now.'

'Then let's get you back to home base,' suggested Greg, throwing his polystyrene mug into the bin. 'You might just catch a couple of hours' sleep before dawn.'

Buffeted by winds and rain, they finally made it back in

Greg's Discovery to a slumbering hotel. Greg thanked them and promised he would be in contact in a few days with news of the Harvills.

Luckily, a sympathetic night porter was there to greet them. 'I'll bring something from the kitchen up to your room,' he promised. 'Just give me a minute or two.'

The irony was that Abbie never saw him again. The next morning she discovered she had collapsed on the bed and fallen asleep in her bath robe before sustenance had arrived!

Word must have got round, Abbie realised a few days later, that she and Matt had been away together for the weekend, as Greg's arrival on the following Tuesday morning caused more than a ripple of interest amongst the staff.

Stephanie, Rachel and Jill sat in the staffroom and plied Greg with pastries from the bakery as he waited for Abbie and Matt to finish their surgeries. Even Frank Morgan seemed to have got wind of their adventure.

Happily Anita Harvill had recovered, and James too, and there was an official letter of thanks from Greg's superiors.

'Do you fancy a repeat performance some time?' Matt asked her that night as they dined on omelette and salad in his kitchen.

'I'd love it.' She managed to laugh. 'Minus the Mickelsdale incident.'

He reached across the table and took her hands, smoothing the soft flesh of her palms with a slow finger. The candles had burnt low and the creamy light flickered around the kitchen. 'Do you mind very much? he asked softly as he looked up at her.

She frowned. 'What about?'

'Well, I'd planned a kind of luxurious castaway weekend but we spent most of it scrabbling around on a storm-tossed hillside.'

Abbie looked down at her hands wrapped between

Matt's strong, tanned fingers. They were so unlike Sean's. A little jolt of remembrance came back as she recalled that Sean's artistic fingers had been slender and had had freckles and tiny fair hairs over their backs.

Matt squeezed her hands and, standing up, pulled her up from her chair and drew her against his chest. 'I know I'm on call, but do you think we could risk going to bed for a few hours?'

She smiled. 'The moment we climb those stairs you know the phone will ring.'

'I'm willing to take the gamble.' He kissed her neck with light, biting kisses and she closed her eyes, losing herself momentarily in the warm wave of pleasure that flowed through her body. Had it been at the lakeside when she had begun to feel differently about him? Had it been then she had known that what she shared with him was quite unlike the relationship she had shared with Sean? Or had it been in that storm on Skiddrigg when she had felt Matt's presence beside her on the hillside that things had begun to clarify in her mind? Had it been since then that she had known how much he had begun to mean to her?

She disentangled herself and began to move some of the dishes to the sink. As she squeezed washing-up liquid over the plates and ran the warm water, Matt joined her.

Placing his hands lightly on her shoulders, he whispered with a tenderness that almost broke her heart, 'Don't shut me out, Abbie.'

She swallowed, keeping her face averted. 'I don't mean to.'

He turned her slowly to face him, lifting her chin to his direct gaze. 'Abbie, what is it?' Just as he spoke the pager in his shirt pocket reverberated against his chest and he lifted his eyes to the ceiling. 'Perfect timing,' he groaned. 'I'll have to call in.'

She smiled, managing to sound casual. 'Saved by the pager, Dr Carrig.'

'Was I getting too close for comfort?' he asked perceptively.

She avoided his searching gaze and turned back to the washing-up. 'I'll finish the clearing for you. Then I should go home.'

'When will I see you next?'

'Are you on call this weekend?'

'Until Sunday night.'

She nodded, swallowing again on the hard lump in her throat as he kissed her cheek and whispered that he would miss her.

On Friday afternoon Jackie Dunn, the district nurse, sat at Abbie's desk and placed Jasper Macdonald's care plan between them. 'Well, here it is,' she sighed, raising her eyebrows, 'though I don't know how long Mr Macdonald will let us keep seeing him.'

Abbie studied the notes, reading the comments the health visitor and social worker had made and finally the observations of Jackie herself who, at almost retiring age, was a mother of four strapping boys and had personal experience of dealing with truculent males. Even so, the last few weeks with Jasper had not been easy.

'We have at least persuaded him to have some help in the house. Other than that, he maintains he doesn't want me visiting, the old buffoon. He says he'll come in to the surgery if he needs help.'

Abbie frowned. 'That's what he said last time.'

'He's as stubborn as a mule.'

Abbie smiled. 'As stubborn as a *deaf* mule.'

They both laughed and Jackie got up and tucked the notes back in her case. 'Well, I'll keep on persevering until he flatly refuses to let me in. At the moment I just hammer on the door until he gives in. That old house could do with a good doorbell. It would save a lot of trouble. Sometimes I even have to traipse around the back and knock on a window.'

Abbie smiled. 'Jasper's probably hopeful you'll get fed up and go away.'

'Well, he's got another think coming,' said Jackie stoutly. 'Oh, I also saw Mr Haskins yesterday,' Jackie went on, 'your seventy-two-year-old pensioner with angina. He's much better after his gastric upset and he's still not smoking.'

Abbie smiled. 'Determined to cram in thirty more darts finals, I expect.'

Jackie frowned. 'What's that?'

'I'll tell you later,' Abbie said, and grinned. 'Oh, will you let me know how you get on with Jasper?'

Jackie nodded. 'I'll keep you posted.'

'Thanks, Jackie.'

Abbie still had a smile on her face at the thought of Arthur Haskins when her next patient entered. 'Hello, Dr Ashby. I don't know if you remember me...?'

Abbie nodded. 'Yes, of course I do, Marion. Sit down.'

Dave Carter's girlfriend took a seat and smiled nervously. 'I wondered if you'd recognise me. You were very kind that day at the hospital.'

'How is Dave?' Abbie asked.

Marion Foster hesitated. 'That's what I've come about. He's being discharged next week...and...' Her face went red and to Abbie's surprise she burst into tears.

'What's wrong?' Abbie asked in concern.

Marion blew her nose with a tissue that Abbie handed her.

'So, what is the problem?' Abbie probed as Marion mopped her tears.

'I'm p-pregnant.' Marion looked up, her lips quivering.

'Are you sure?'

The girl nodded. 'I've been on the Pill while I've been seeing Dave. I just don't know what happened. Perhaps it was when I had flu.'

'Have you missed a period?'

Marion gazed down at her lap. 'Yes, two. Until I went on the Pill I've always been irregular so I didn't worry too much at first, but then I began to get morning sickness. My last period was about twelve weeks ago so I did a home test and it was positive.'

Abbie lifted her eyebrows. 'Are you registered with us?'

'No, I live in Hobcraig. Dr Wesley's our doctor. But I'd like to see you now as you know what's been happening with Dave and me. Oh, and there will be Jonathan to register, too.'

'Who is Jonathan?' Abbie asked in confusion.

Marion looked up. 'My son. He's only three.' She added, swallowing hard. 'Dave isn't his father.'

The bits of the puzzle of Dave's and Marion's relationship began to fit together, Abbie thought as she remembered what Marion had said about her home life and her over-protective parents.

'I had Jonathan at sixteen,' Marion went on. 'His father never admitted responsibility. He was only sixteen too. That's why my parents moved down from the border, to get a fresh start in Hobcraig.' She stopped, trying hard to regain her composure.

Abbie gave the girl time to blow her nose again, then nodded. 'I see. Well, I can agree to accept you and Jonathan as patients if that's what you want.'

Marion nodded firmly. 'Yes, definitely. Dr Wesley doesn't know us very well anyway.'

'All right, I'll get the paperwork arranged. Meanwhile, pop off your undies and climb onto the examination bench for me, will you, Marion?'

Abbie went out to Reception to collect the relevant paperwork. Hesitant as she was to accept Dr Wesley's patient, having come this far, she felt obliged to continue in view of the situation.

'Have you discussed the situation with Dave?' Abbie asked as she began her examination.

'No. How could I, with him still in hospital? I told Mum and she told Dad and he was furious. I suppose after Jonathan it's only natural.'

'Don't you think you should have waited to break the news to Dave first?' Abbie queried.

The small, fair head nodded. 'It's too late now. The damage is done.'

'By the look of it, you're about right,' Abbie commented as she completed her examination and gestured for Marion to sit upright.

'You mean I am pregnant?'

'Yes, though we'll have to confirm it and calculate the date but you're probably right at about three months.'

The girl stood in silence, biting on her bottom lip. 'Just when I was beginning to think everything was going to get better. I've even got a job I like at a nursing home.'

'What do you do there?' Abbie asked.

'Auxiliary nursing. I really like the old folk, but I suppose I'll have to give it up, won't I?'

'Well, you won't be able to do any heavy lifting,' Abbie warned. 'Light jobs only from now on.'

The tears glimmered at the corner of her patient's eyes. Softly, Marion began to weep again.

One day the following week Abbie peered into Michele's open mouth and discovered a full-blown case of tonsillitis.

'It hurts,' Michele complained again. 'And my neck aches, Aunt Abbie.'

'How often is she going to have these attacks?' Joely

asked, replacing the ice cream Michele had refused to eat with a long, cool drink of mineral water. 'Can't she have her tonsils removed?'

They were sitting on the edge of Michele's bed and Abbie looked at the swollen lymph nodes that had appeared in her niece's neck. 'We hesitate to remove them now,' she explained. 'They form part of the body's lymphatic system. Michele's tonsils are an important part of her defence system.'

'But I had to have mine removed,' her sister pointed out. 'And I remember going for days with a sore throat before then. Do you think Michele is going to have the same trouble?'

Abbie glanced at her niece's flushed face on the white pillow and tucked the sheet up to her chin. 'Not necessarily.' She smiled at Michele. 'I'll give you something to help your sore throat, darling, but until it works keep warm and cosy in bed.'

Michele managed a smile. 'Mummy said I can watch *Blue Peter* later if I'm better.'

Abbie nodded. 'Have forty winks first, though.'

Downstairs, in the kitchen, Joely made them coffee and they sat at the breakfast bar to drink it. 'I hesitate to give an antibiotic,' Abbie sighed, 'but I don't think we have any choice here.'

Joely nodded, folding the prescription up and slipping it into her purse. 'Mum's calling by later. I'll pop out then and get it from the chemist.'

'I would call in after surgery, but it will be rather late,' Abbie said as she sipped her coffee. 'No doubt you'll want some shopping.'

'No.' Joely shrugged. 'Phil's bringing in some groceries. He's having supper here tonight.' Joely smiled at her sister's thoughtful face. 'Don't worry, Abs, Phil is a lovely man, but I'm not going to make any more daft mistakes like I did with Michele's father.'

Abbie felt a pang of sympathy for her sister as she thought of the desperate moments after Michele had discovered her pregnancy, the boy having disappeared after a brief interlude of time. It had been tragic for Joely but even more so for Michele who would never know her real father. And yet Michele had filled their lives with such happiness that it was impossible to imagine not having her.

Taking leave of her sister and niece, Abbie drove back to the surgery and recalled the days of Joely's youth. Joely had been a happy-go-lucky teenager and she herself newly married to Sean. But the accident had caused their relationship to change. Abbie had been forced to assume a position of responsibility and Joely, after Michele's birth, had not been the carefree youngster she had once been. At last, however, time seemed to have brought happiness for Joely, and Abbie hoped that Phil would turn out to be the right man.

On impulse Abbie turned her car towards Jasper Macdonald's house. As she parked the car in the drive, she saw the door open. Jasper stood there, and though looking frail, he was smiling.

'Just a social call,' Abbie said quickly as he led her into the hall.

Jasper turned a wry smile on her. 'You're checking up on me, no doubt, like that other woman.'

'You mean Jackie?' Abbie sat down in the sitting room, unable to hide her amusement. 'The poor woman's only trying to be helpful.'

'Well, I've done without women's fussing so far, I'll be jiggered if I have to put up with it now,' Jasper answered unequivocally.

Abbie knew that both Jackie and Jasper had wills of iron

and it took no stretch of imagination to guess there were sparks flying between them.

Jasper sank into a chair. 'You'll be calling at the cottage in the next road?' he asked as he made himself comfortable.

Abbie hesitated, then realised it was no use trying to fool her old friend. 'Dr Carrig's leased it while he's here.'

'About time too,' put in Jasper, arching an eyebrow.

'About time for what?' Abbie frowned.

'For you settling down again.'

'Whatever makes you say that?' Abbie blushed.

Jasper grinned, looking more like his old mischievous self. 'A little bird told me.'

'I suppose it was Jackie.' Abbie was unable to think of anyone else who might have informed Jasper.

'Not at all. I got it from the man himself.' He chuckled but his laughter provoked a bout of coughing. When he'd recovered he looked at her and said wheezily, 'I'll let you into a little secret. Your young doctor calls by every now and then and we have a quiet game of backgammon.'

'I had no idea,' she acknowledged. 'He hasn't mentioned it to me.'

'Told him not to,' said Jasper with a defiant flourish. 'Didn't want any of you lot putting ideas into his head about hospices and so forth.'

'Jasper,' Abbie said gently, 'we have your best interests at heart.'

He looked at her and shrugged. 'Yes, lass, but I like my independence.'

Abbie smiled. 'As if we didn't know. So, tell me, have you met your match at backgammon yet?'

'Very nearly,' remarked Jasper with a wink. 'He's a canny player all right. First decent game I've had since the last one I had with your father. You know, those two would have got along well.'

Abbie took a deep breath, realising he was right, but the little pain under her ribs prevented her from commenting.

Sensing that he had struck home, Jasper leaned back in his chair. 'So,' he muttered, fixing her with an incisive stare, 'what are you going to do about him, girl?'

It was a question that left Abbie with only one answer. 'There's nothing I can do,' she replied truthfully. 'He leaves England later in the year and that, Jasper, is the end of it.'

CHAPTER SEVEN

SEVEN-week-old Monica Kay gurgled up at Abbie. 'She's feeding well, by the looks of her. I don't think you have any cause for worry, Serena,' Abbie remarked as she tickled the pink tummy, drawing more happy gurgles from the little girl. 'Your breasts are healthy and so is Monica.'

'I hope I'll be able to breast-feed for a long time yet,' said Serena, pulling on her blouse and buttoning it up. 'But Monica never seems to have enough. Do you think I'm providing her with what she needs?'

Abbie tucked the tiny vest into place and ran her fingers over Monica's legs. 'Every woman is physically capable of providing milk, but the let-down reflex may be inhibited if you are stressed or anxious.'

Serena frowned. 'The let-down reflex?'

'Milk is released,' Abbie explained, 'when stimulated by a reflex, for instance just thinking about a feed or hearing Monica cry. The pituitary gland triggers a reflex, which releases a hormone called oxytocin.'

'But I thought the milk was already there in the breast,' Serena said. 'And when the baby sucks it automatically comes.'

'It is there,' Abbie agreed, 'but the oxytocin causes the muscles surrounding the milk-producing cells to contract. It's only then that the milk glands empty milk into the reservoirs behind the nipple ready for the baby to drink.'

'So you're saying that if I'm stressed, this whole cycle of events is interrupted?'

Abbie nodded. 'It's a bit of a vicious circle, I'm afraid. Is there anything in particular that's worrying you?'

Serena sighed as she took Monica from Abbie and re-dressed her in a pink romper suit. 'I suppose I'm just an anxious older mother. When you're in your twenties, you take everything in your stride. When you are closer to your forties, and you've been trying for a baby for so long everything seems magnified.' She looked up and smiled at Abbie. 'But I would have been much more anxious if it hadn't been for Dr Carrig's clinic. It's a lifeline for me. I've met other mothers there who had babies late in life, one lady in particular who has a dear little girl called Katey Marsh. She reads from a book to Monica whilst we're waiting.'

Abbie laughed. 'Oh, yes. *What Katey Did in the Kitchen*.

Serena nodded. 'Mrs Marsh said that Dr Carrig suggested the book for her. It's been very helpful with Katey's weight problem.'

Abbie nodded. 'We don't advise diets as such for children, but recommend healthy eating. Apparently the book is working.'

'Well, she looks fine to me,' Serena remarked. 'And have you noticed Monica's foot?'

Abbie took Monica, now fully dressed, in her arms again and coaxed a wide grin from her. 'It's well on the mend, isn't it?' The talipes was disappearing, the tiny limb becoming extended in the normal fashion.

'Thanks to all the exercises Dr Carrig showed us. If we hadn't given Monica the physiotherapy so early there would have been a good chance of her not walking properly. He's so good with children and babies. Is he married?'

'No,' Abbie replied quietly.

'And never has been?'

Abbie grinned, passing Monica back to her mother. 'Not that he's mentioned.'

Serena gave Abbie an innocent look. 'He'll make a fine husband for someone one day, don't you think?'

Abbie refrained from commenting and as Serena rose to go Abbie couldn't help feeling a little irritated. Everyone these days seemed to be hinting at the relationship between her and Matt. Was she going to have to put up a luminous sign in Reception that he was in no way a permanent member of staff? Of course, she wouldn't, but it was irking that so many patients made this assumption after having been told exactly what the position was.

It was as she was accompanying Serena to the waiting room that she bumped into Matt, talking to Marion Foster and Dave Carter. Abbie had finished her surgery for the afternoon, but as Marion walked across the room she wasn't surprised when the young woman asked if she could speak to her.

'I know we haven't made an appointment,' she said anxiously. 'but we need to talk someone, Dr Ashby. Dr Carrig's has been talking to us...'

Abbie glanced at Serena and said goodbye, before turning her attention back to Marion. 'Then I'll leave you with him, shall I? Obviously you only want one of us.'

Marion looked startled. 'It was Dave, you see,' she mumbled apologetically. 'He feels Dr Carrig would understand his position while I prefer to see you.'

'Well, you'll have to decide or come to us separately,' Abbie said, relenting a little.

'Couldn't we, just this time, speak to you both?' asked her patient. 'It took so much persuading to get Dave here.'

Abbie glanced at Matt and Dave Carter who were deep in conversation. 'You'd better come in,' she said, 'providing Dr Carrig hasn't a patient waiting for him.'

'Oh, thank you, Dr Ashby,' sighed Marion. 'I promise we won't do it again.'

Abbie led the way back into her room and, glancing over her shoulder, saw that Marion, Dave and Matt were following. Matt gave her a slight shrug as he walked past and Abbie closed the door.

Abbie gestured to the two chairs at the side of her desk and the couple sat down, but Matt propped himself against the wall, folding his arms across his chest.

'Dave still has headaches,' Marion began, and Abbie noted the scar on the side of his face which, although it had healed, would probably remain visible for some time.

'And the arm?' she enquired of a somewhat silent Dave.

He pulled up his sweater sleeve to reveal a corrective splint bound to his wrist. 'They've given me this to wear. They said it will realign the soft tissue and correct any deformities. But I can't go back to work.'

Both Marion and Dave fell silent again. Abbie glanced at Matt who raised his eyebrows, peeled himself off the wall and walked to the desk. 'Is there any improvement in your situation at home?' he asked Marion.

'I just wish I could make them see how much I love Dave,' Marion blurted out, her eyes filling with tears, 'but they've become so protective of Jonathan. It's like I don't have a life any more. I know it was through me they had to move before, but all I want them to do is give us a chance. While they're so angry with me I just can't think straight.'

Dave looked at Matt, then at Abbie. 'I can understand their reaction. There's a big age difference between us. Marion's only nineteen and I shall be thirty-one soon. And…' He paused, glancing at Marion. 'I've been married before and I've no real security to offer. I can understand they don't want her to make another big mistake.'

'Perhaps,' suggested Abbie, 'it's a better idea just to let Marion's parents get used to the idea for a while. It's been a shock for them, but once they know you intend to provide some security they'll come around.'

'And that's just the problem,' Dave muttered as she obviously struck home with the remark. 'There's practically no accommodation in Rendale, certainly not during the summer. It doesn't help with me off sick either.'

'I don't want it adopted,' Marion suddenly sobbed. 'I just couldn't—I couldn't!'

Dave looked stricken, then rose and knelt to take her hand in his. 'Marion, is that what you've been thinking?'

She nodded. 'I thought you didn't want me, or the baby. I know I've left it late to think about an abortion…'

'You won't talk to me,' Dave argued gently, looking up into her face. 'You won't say a word.'

Matt moved forward, frowning. 'I think you must work out some kind of plan,' he said quietly but firmly. 'Discuss what it is you both want, then stick to it. Remain united in your decision.'

Abbie looked at Matt and knew that nothing more could be said on their part. The decision on the baby's future was theirs alone. She felt sympathetic towards the couple, but there was little more she could do.

'Come back when you have talked things over,' she said quietly, and the couple rose, Marion wiping her cheeks with a tissue and Dave looking bewildered.

That evening, as Abbie walked with Matt in the woods which had become their special place, she expressed her concern for Dave and Marion.

'They need to find somewhere to live,' said Matt practically. 'Give them a base to work from. Is he in danger of losing his job, do you think?'

'He's a temporary sports coach. Obviously the activity centre won't pay him for very much longer,' sighed Abbie. 'It's not the brightest of outlooks.'

'You say he's been married before?'

Abbie nodded. 'It must be worrying for Marion's parents too. Jonathan means a great deal to them.'

'But he isn't *their* son,' Matt remarked as they came to

a clearing. 'He's their grandson and it's important to remember their roles in all this.'

'Grandparents don't suddenly have lesser feelings of responsibility,' Abbie protested. 'They've looked after him for three years.'

He nodded. 'But sooner or later their daughter has to assert her independence. It's Marion's choice as Jonathan's mother,' Matt pointed out, 'to decide whether she wants to create her own family or keep anchored to the parental circle. What was she—sixteen when she had the child? And now there's another baby on the way. It seems plain to me that she must make her own home both for her and her parents' sake.'

'Are you suggesting it's best for her to leave a secure environment for an unknown one?'

'I'm merely saying it's time for her to take the responsibility for her actions.' He tilted Abbie's chin up and bent his head, kissing her softly. 'Now, let's go home,' he whispered, and she nodded, suddenly wanting to be held closely and know that home for her was, and would always be, the warm circle of his arms.

'Darling, you're looking peaky this last week or so,' Bonnie observed as she studied the recumbent form of her elder daughter. Abbie lay in a deck chair, a straw hat tilted over her face against the sun. She had fought off the flu, she hoped, which had brought several of her patients to the surgery this last week.

She had also changed the contraceptive Pill that she had been taking, which had seemed to unsettle her. Not having had to bother with the Pill for so many years until meeting Matt, she realised that her body needed to make adjustments. Hopefully the one that she was now taking would prove acceptable for the short period she would be on it.

It was a balmy Sunday afternoon at the beginning of

July, and Abbie and her mother had spent the last few hours tidying the garden. That evening, Bonnie had arranged a small dinner party for six. The event, Bonnie had told them, was to celebrate a surprise.

Abbie felt anxious. She and Matt had differed in their opinions over Jasper, who had flatly refused to allow Jackie into his house any more. Jackie had sought support from Abbie, who in turn had approached Matt who appeared to have the golden touch with Jasper. But Matt had merely shrugged and told them both to leave well enough alone.

'But that's quite irresponsible!' Jackie had exclaimed angrily as the three of them had gathered in the office. 'He needs DN support and it's my job to see that he has it. How do we know his hygiene isn't suffering for a start?'

'Has he asked you for help with baths?' Matt had asked quietly.

'Well, no, but all the same—'

'Then why not wait until he does?' Matt had appeared to brush off a problem which had been, to Jackie, tantamount to dereliction of duty.

'He'll come around.' Matt had shrugged. 'In his own time.'

'Which could be too late,' Jackie had protested reasonably. 'Look at how Abbie found him when he had that last infection!'

'I'll keep an eye on him,' Matt had said with a reasonable air that had annoyed the nurse.

'Well, if I'm to be redundant—fine!' muttered Jackie as she left the room.

Matt looked at Abbie as the door closed behind her. 'What have I said?' he asked blankly.

'Jackie has only a year left in nursing,' she said with a sigh. 'She dreads the thought of giving up. And, besides, she has a point.'

'Does she expect to force her way into Jasper's house?' Matt asked sharply.

'No, of course not. But Jackie is only doing what she feels is her duty.'

'Abbie, we aren't still living in the days of Florence Nightingale. We can relax the rules a bit now.' He shrugged and Abbie bit her lip.

Jackie meant well, but she was a little overbearing and her strong personality sometimes aggravated some of the less timid of their patients, like Jasper. However, Abbie had known Jackie for a long time and she was a good nurse.

There was no resolution to the problem that day and Abbie dragged back her thoughts to the moment as her mother rested back on her heels, shielding the sun from her eyes.

'Are you sure you feel well enough for the party?' her mother asked as she studied her daughter's pale face.

Abbie nodded. 'I'll be fine.'

'The trouble is, you don't relax enough.' Bonnie looked at her with sympathy. 'You drive yourself too hard. You always did, even when Dad was alive. Even more so when you married Sean.'

Abbie shrugged. 'In those days we were building up the practice.'

Her mother smiled. 'I know. But I often wondered—' She lifted her shoulders on a sigh. 'I'd hoped that we would be grandparents one day.'

Abbie was silent. She had wanted that too. More than anything she had wanted a child. She nodded slowly. 'Yes, I would have wished that for you too.'

'I suppose it was not to be,' her mother said, and met Abbie's gaze. 'Though I knew that you wanted a family, darling.'

'Oh, Mum…' Abbie drew her hands over her face, then looked up, her eyes confused. 'I wanted a baby more than anything, but Sean was never happy about the idea. He said he wanted to wait until we were settled, but I began to realise that he had no desire for a family.'

'And it became a problem in your relationship?'

Abbie nodded. 'Yes. I'm afraid so.'

'Darling, I'm sorry.'

Abbie shrugged again. 'I don't know if we would have ever overcome that problem, or even, if Sean had agreed to having a child, whether it would have narrowed the distance between us.'

Bonnie was silent for a moment before she spoke. 'Your support brought Joely and I through the dark times, darling,' her mother said softly. 'Now you have found some happiness with Matt. Enjoy it.'

As she sat there, Abbie felt a desperate urgency to see Matt, to absorb his presence. She rose from the deckchair, glancing at her wristwatch. 'Perhaps we should think about getting some food ready for this evening?'

Bonnie's eyes opened wide. 'Oh, my goodness, I'd almost forgotten—dinner!'

'What if I prepare starters and you do the main course?'

'Wonderful,' her mother agreed. 'And while we are about it, shouldn't we test the wine?'

They both laughed as they walked towards the house. 'Red or white or both?' asked Abbie teasingly.

'Champagne,' responded Bonnie immediately. A remark which left Abbie wondering what new turn of events lay ahead of them that evening.

It was the kind of soft summer's evening made for lovers, Abbie thought as she slipped on a simple black, sleeveless, evening frock. Teaming it with shiny black high heels and small pearl earrings, it looked absolutely right, she thought as she examined her reflection critically in her bedroom mirror.

Turning several times in front of it, she dabbed on her usual perfume, and then went to stand at her window to breathe in the scents from the garden below. Abbie leaned her elbows on the sill and gazed out at the night. Her jade eyes reflected the scene below—the terrace bathed in a pool of warmth, the stone hoarding the heat still shimmering over its surface. Beyond were the trees and borders and their exotic, almost tropical scents. Pushing back her coppery hair, freshly washed and dried into a bob, she breathed in once more, closing her eyes.

Her moment of reverie was shattered as the front doorbell chimed loudly in the hall below. Abbie glanced at her reflection for the last time and smoothed down her dress, before going downstairs. As she opened the door her heart gave a leap of recognition at the tall, dark and amazingly handsome man standing on the doorstep.

He wore a silk black bow tie and formal dark suit, and before she could speak he had taken her in his arms, his lips coming down to kiss her with a need that she also felt. 'Oh, Abbie,' Matt whispered, as his breath fanned her cheek, 'I've missed you.'

'Me, too,' she whispered back. His voice was heavy with desire and she felt the muscles in her stomach tighten. As Bonnie called out from the kitchen they broke apart and Abbie closed the front door.

'Do you know what the surprise is?' he asked, his voice returning to its normal deep quality as he handed her a bottle of expensive-looking wine.

'No, but I think I can guess,' she answered, and slid her hand into his, leading him towards the dining room.

Bonnie's surprise delighted everyone.

When the delicious dinner of melon cocktail, griddled chicken and crêpes Suzettes was over, and they were gathered in the conservatory, Bonnie broke open the bottle of champagne.

When everyone's glass was full, she faced her guests. Abbie sat next to Matt on the comfortable rattan settee and Joely and Phil were reclining on the steamer chairs by the window. They had found a babysitter for the evening and as Michele had fully recovered from the bout of tonsillitis, they were in relaxed and happy mood.

'You've all been very patient,' she told them as, smoothing down her pretty plum-coloured dress, she looked at the silver-haired man beside her dressed in a smart dark suit. 'Don and I have an announcement to make. We wanted to celebrate in a very special way.'

Everyone looked at Don. Abbie met Joely's glance and saw that she was grinning. Joely suspected what she herself did—an engagement announcement. She glanced at Matt, meeting his gaze, and realised that he, too, was thinking the same.

Bonnie lifted her glass of champagne. 'I would like you all to wish Don and me success. Last week we became partners.'

There was an audible gasp in the room. Then Don stood up beside Bonnie and chinked his glass against hers.

'Between us,' he told them, 'we have bought the lease on the little souvenir shop in the high street. With a little luck and a fair breeze, we shall be opening the door to custom in three weeks' time!'

Later that night, Abbie lay wrapped safely in Matt's arms. The moon shone through the bedroom window with a clear, sparkling light that fell on the glossy silk folds of her castoff dress. It lay where it had fallen across the little white wicker chair which she had painted shortly after Matt had moved in. Above it hung a print by a Renaissance artist of a knight in armour, sweeping his beautiful conquest into his arms.

Matt moved beside her, their love-making having ended in an exhausted peace filled with the wonder of being alone together and the need to do nothing and say nothing, but just lie in each other's arms.

Abbie had missed the contours of Matt's strong, lean body with a hunger that alarmed her. She loved the jut of masculine hip and firm, flat stomach that now lay against the column of her spine as he wrapped his arms around her, breathing as one with her, tranquil and even.

'That was wonderful,' he whispered against her ear, 'but now I feel guilty for having whisked you away from the party.'

He had given her so much pleasure she had forgotten anything else but the world in which they lay. 'I think Mum and Don were only too happy to have some time to themselves,' she said, turning to snuggle against his warm hard chest.

'Mmm. That's nice. Your hair smells of flowers.'

'Lemon, actually.'

'Is it?' His voice was deep and reassuring above her, blending into the darkness as though it were melting there, fusing with the shadows. She loved his voice, his deep rumble of laughter, his sexy groans. 'Whatever it is, I'm hooked.' He brushed the top of her head with his mouth, breathing into her hair. 'So what did you think of your mother's surprise?' he asked softly.

'I was surprised,' Abbie admitted ruefully. 'Weren't you?'

'Absolutely. But thrilled for them. I think they make perfect business partners. They've got the right temperaments.'

'But not...' Abbie hesitated. '...Not as husband and wife?'

'Oh, I think that will come eventually.'

'Do you?' Abbie sighed softly. 'I wonder.'

'No one will replace your father,' Matt murmured above her. 'That's perfectly clear. But I don't think Don intends to.'

'I think they'll be very happy,' Abbie murmured as Matt's hands travelled up and down her spine.

He kissed her and whispered, 'As the song goes, that's what love does for you.'

Abbie didn't reply. She had no need, for she knew very well what love could do…. Had known for some time…that love had changed her life.

CHAPTER EIGHT

Two weeks into July, the weather changed. The sun vanished into a sky that seemed locked in permanent cloud. The rain, gentle at first, escalated into a downpour similar to that of the May weekend which had claimed the Harvills as its victims on Mickelsdale Fell.

The only advantage of a tourist town in summer lost under a glassy sea of rain, Abbie thought, was that not even the temporary residents cared to emerge to come to a doctor's surgery.

The rain relented slightly on the day of the opening of Blotters. Bonnie, untroubled by the inclement weather, dispensed glasses of white wine to all her customers. Matt, Frank and Abbie spent their lunch-hour at the shop, before returning to the surgery in the afternoon.

Blotters was packed and Abbie was thrilled for her mother. Bonnie and Don had put a lot of work into the shop over the last few weeks, redecorating and restocking. It was clear that Bonnie, dressed in a smart suit and with a fashionable hairstyle, was in her element.

'This is just what I want!' exclaimed one satisfied customer, lifting a small hand-crafted owl sculpture from the shelf. 'And very reasonable too,' she whispered to her friend.

'I'll also take one,' replied the woman eagerly. 'My niece collects birds. It'll be just right for her.'

Abbie gazed proudly at her mother, who was operating the computer and its accompanying till.

'Something tells me this place is going to be a roaring success,' Matt said quietly as he stood beside Abbie.

'I can hardly believe the change in Mum lately,' agreed Abbie.

'She seems to be a natural,' Matt observed.

Abbie nodded. 'Mum was always nervous of technology. She's not fazed by any of it now.'

'Abbie!' someone called across the crowded room, and Abbie looked up to see her sister, signalling from the doorway.

'Aunt Abbie, look what Grandma has given me!' Michele, dressed in her Spice Girls T-shirt, reached her first, holding up a tiny china figure for her to see. 'It's Badger from *Wind in the Willows*.'

'You'll be able to start a collection.' Abbie lifted her niece into her arms as Phil and Joely joined them. 'With Grandma owning a shop, perhaps you'll be able to ask for a special discount.'

Everyone laughed and Don, who was serving a customer, looked over his shoulder and called, 'There's a ten per cent discount today for everyone so take the opportunity while you can.' He gave them a wink and turned back to his customer.

'An offer I can't refuse.' Joely giggled. 'I'm going to buy one of those little silver snuff boxes over there. Come on, Phil.'

Phil grimaced. 'I thought there might be a catch.'

After purchasing a pretty frosted glass bell, Abbie made her way back to Matt who was talking to a lady in a red jumper. She gave him a beaming smile and hurried off to the cash desk.

'I've just sold her that teapot,' Matt whispered in Abbie's ear. 'Do we get commission too?'

Abbie pulled a face. 'No, you might get a cup of tea, though. That is, if we manage to get back to the surgery in time.'

He slid his hand around her waist. 'Just when I was having fun.'

On the way out Abbie bent to kiss Michele and say good-bye to her sister and Phil. As Matt and Phil talked, Bonnie came over and, drawing Abbie aside, thanked her for coming. 'It was wonderful to have Matt here too,' she said as they both glanced across the crowded room to where Matt and Phil were talking.

Abbie nodded, her heart giving a little jump as she looked, unobserved, at Matt's tall, dark figure. 'He thinks you'll make a great success of this, Mum.'

'I hope so,' Bonnie said quietly. 'I'm very fond of Matt,' she added, and Abbie looked at her and suddenly realised how much a part of everyone's life Matt had become. She hadn't considered that before, and as Michele squeezed her way through the crowd to join Phil and Matt, talking excitedly as she raised a small china ballerina to show them, Abbie swallowed.

'I'd better go, Mum. Good luck with the rest of the day,' she said quickly, and as she bent to kiss her mother on the cheek she saw that Matt had picked up Michele in his arms in order that she might reach onto the shelf above her head to replace the figurine.

For a moment she saw Michele's small arm around his broad shoulders, her small face break into smiles as he made her laugh, then, as he gently lowered her to the floor, the brief second where she looked up at him and he at her. The moment seemed captured in time and was as painful as it was poignant.

She glanced back at her mother whose expression revealed that she had caught the moment too. Unable to speak without giving herself away, Abbie smiled and turned to push her way through to the door.

Once outside, Matt caught her up, by which time she had managed to compose herself, swift to recollect all the things that she had held dear in her life before Matt had come along. Yes, she did value her independence. Yes, she had come to terms with her life and career after Sean's death and yes, she was perfectly content with her role of Michele's beloved aunt.

But the moment in the shop had caught her unawares, and as she tried to make conversation with Matt while they walked to their cars she could not ignore the fact that it had shaken her more than she cared to admit.

It was a violently blustery Monday when Abbie heard the first forecast of gales. The rain had not really ceased for almost a month and now there were high winds. Despite predictions of a heatwave, the end of July was overcast. Not that it was evident, by the amount of patients that still arrived from the activity centre. Matt's TR surgeries were as busy as ever, but this particular Monday he knocked on Abbie's door and she knew there was something amiss as soon as she looked into his eyes.

'Have you seen the list for house calls yet?' he asked her.

'No,' she admitted, closing her diary and standing up. 'Why, are we inundated?'

'I thought I should show you this.' He handed her the notes written by Stephanie. 'It's a visit phoned in about ten minutes ago. The man requested Frank.'

Abbie read the name at the top of the page and a sense of dread went through her. She forced herself to continue reading, digesting the notes that Stephanie had made.

'"Gwyneth Kilerne, stomach pains",' she eventually read aloud. She looked up at Matt and cleared her throat. 'The Kilernes aren't people to ask for a visit if they can avoid it.'

'No, I gathered as much.'

Abbie frowned. 'Did you?'

'Jasper mentioned them—in connection with the accident your father and husband were involved in.'

Abbie looked down at the desk. 'What exactly did Jasper tell you?'

'Only that the Kilernes are difficult people,' he said quietly. Then, sinking down into the chair opposite her, he added, 'Abbie, I'm coming with you.'

'It isn't necessary for two of us to go,' she said unable to hide a tremor in her voice. She kept her face averted, feeling cool perspiration break out along the line of her forehead. She stood up and, reaching for her mac, began to pull it on. 'I'm quite capable of making a half-hour journey, thanks all the same.'

'It won't be a half-hour journey, will it?' Matt pointed out, rising to his feet. 'More like an hour in this weather. Have you heard the forecast?'

'I'll be careful. Don't worry.'

'Abbie?' He barred the way as she turned to the door. 'You haven't driven up there since the accident, have you?'

She met his gaze and shook her head. No…no, I haven't.'

'Esk Fell is notorious in bad weather,' he went on, his eyes going slowly over her face. 'The wind is up to sixty miles an hour in some places. I know you are quite capable of making the journey, but if it were anyone else intending to drive up there in these conditions, I would say the same.'

She knew he was right. Esk Fell was a switchback of roads and narrow bends. Only the odd farm broke the wilderness of that brooding countryside.

Donovan Kilerne and his wife, to give them their due, rarely called for assistance. The last time they had done so, Gwyneth had miscarried and Abbie's father and Sean had driven to their deaths on the return journey. Since then she had waited for the call that might one day take her again to the remote farmhouse, but it had never come.

In five years the couple had become recluse so she had seen them once, two years ago, when Gwyneth had been driven to the surgery by Donovan in their old truck. The atmosphere had been cool and it had left Abbie with a feeling of deep dismay.

'I'll grab my case and I'll meet you at the car,' he said in a tone brooking no further argument. And with that he left her, her protest dying on her lips.

It was a battle even to get to the Citroën, but Matt was beside her, his arm firmly around Abbie's shoulders, steadying her against the wind. Once inside the car, he started the wipers. Debris from the trees littered the window and he was forced to climb out again and remove the accumulation of branches and twigs jamming the windscreen.

As he sank back into his seat and slammed the door he frowned, peering up at the malevolent sky. 'It's not going to blow itself out, that's for sure. They said something about a force ten on the coast during the night. Let's hope we escape the worst.'

Abbie clicked in her safety belt and frowned out at the damp, wind-blown streets as Matt drove from the car park through a deserted Rendale. 'Did Donovan say what he thought could be wrong with Gwyneth?' she asked.

'Stephanie didn't know. Only that their truck has broken down and they couldn't make it in.'

Abbie sat back with a sigh. 'What else did Jasper tell you?'

He shrugged. 'Not much.'

Abbie paused, her eyes following the road which led from Rendale and out into the rugged countryside. 'The Kilernes keep sheep and are self-sufficient to a point. They were a childless couple until Gwyneth became pregnant when she was twenty-nine. Dad was her GP.' Abbie took a deep breath, struggling with the painful memory. 'One day, Gwyneth lost her footing on the hillside and fell. By the time Dad and Sean got out there, it was too late. The Kilernes felt, however, that if he had arrived sooner he might have saved the baby.'

Matt glanced across at her. 'Why was Sean with your father?'

'Dad's car had broken down. Sean offered to drive him.'

He returned his concentration to the road. After a while he said, 'You think the Kilernes still bear a grudge after all this time?'

Abbie nodded. 'I believe so.'

'But your father was probably as swift to reach them in the car as an ambulance would have been coming all the way from a hospital.'

'The Kilernes don't see it that way. Unfortunately Dad and Sean couldn't defend themselves. They were…'

He reached out and squeezed her hand. 'Listen to me, Abbie. I'm sure your father and Sean did as much as any doctor could. The Kilernes were obviously upset, but to lay the blame, as they did, is totally unacceptable.'

Abbie gazed out of the window and nodded, biting down on her lip. A blast of rain washed against the glass and she blinked. As it cleared, she recognised the twist of road that signalled the foot of Esk Fell.

Abbie tried to relax but everything about the place brought back memories. The craggy countryside and rain-lashed peaks looked much the same as the rest of the breathtaking hillsides of Cumbria, but there was an innate difference for her. This place had claimed the lives of two people she had loved dearly and had changed her life for good five years ago. She could never forgive it, or forget it.

'Take the left fork in the road,' she told Matt as they came to the first junction. 'Then we'll climb steadily towards the Kilernes'.'

Matt nodded and engaged second gear. He took the narrowing curves with care and avoided the few bedraggled sheep who sheltered at the roadside.

The ascent was steep, with a sheer drop on one side. They slowed to a crawl as he navigated the sharp bends, rain and wind beating savagely against the car.

'Are you OK?' he asked, glancing across at her.

She nodded, her eyes pinned to the next thirty metres of roadside where, since the accident, a metal road barrier had been erected with white and red stripes painted on its interfacing.

Matt seemed to read her thoughts again as he looked at her face and said quietly, 'It was here, wasn't it?'

'Yes.' She nodded, as for a moment she could see nothing, the road and sign hidden behind a gust of wind-driven rain. Eventually they negotiated the corner and left the unhappy place behind them. The remainder of the climb was fraught with squalls of wind and rain, but Matt drove slowly and carefully upwards until they came to a level stretch of road which led to the Kilernes' old farmhouse.

Donovan Kilerne opened the door to Matt's knock, his expression shocked. 'I sent for Frank Morgan,' he complained at once.

'He's not at the surgery today.' Abbie was forced to shout over the wind, and though she had prepared herself for the meeting with Donovan it still came as a shock to discover his hostility.

'I'm Dr Carrig, Dr Ashby's locum.' Matt's raised voice followed Abbie's. 'We are going to be blown away very soon if we stand here much longer.'

The cottage door creaked open and Abbie and Matt stepped in. The room was gloomy, cold and austere. In one corner an armchair had been made up with blankets and pillows. Gwyneth Kilerne lay against them, her face pale under her untidy dark hair. In the middle of the room was a table and four wooden chairs, and behind it a wood-burning stove. A Border collie lay in a basket by the stove, and his ears pricked up at their entrance.

'Hello, Gwyneth,' Abbie said, though the disappointment was evident on the woman's thin, white face.

'I got a stomach ache,' Gwyneth said sourly as Abbie approached. 'Where's Frank Morgan?'

'They've sent *her* instead,' muttered Donovan ungratefully.

'Don't want you touching me!' Glancing from her husband to Abbie, Gwyneth pulled the blanket up to her chin.

Abbie knelt down and was about to pull the blanket back when the woman howled and Gwyneth's head disappeared under the blanket.

Abbie frowned up at Donovan. 'I have to examine her.'

'She don't want you,' he retorted rudely. 'Thought the other one was coming.'

'I told you, Dr Morgan is off duty,' Abbie explained patiently, but the blanket remained firmly in position. Abbie sighed and stood up. 'Will you allow Dr Carrig to have a look at you, Gwyneth?'

''E's not from round here,' said Donovan. 'Don't like strangers.'

'I'm afraid you haven't very much choice,' Matt intervened, lowering his case to the floor. 'Now, what's it to be, Mrs Kilerne? Lower the blanket or we'll have to be on our way.'

After a few seconds, the blanket lowered. Gwyneth looked up at Matt, her eyes suspicious. Matt knelt on one knee and drew the blanket back. 'Now, where is the pain?' he asked briskly.

Grunting, Donovan Kilerne shuffled away and Matt was left to examined Gwyneth's swollen stomach. Even before he spoke Abbie guessed that their patient was pregnant. She also guessed that Matt was silently assessing the height of the uterus and the size and position of the baby, and that by the look on his face he had detected the foetal heartbeat. Finally he removed his stethoscope and looked at Gwyneth. 'You know you are pregnant, don't you, Mrs Kilerne?'

A stifled gasp came from the other side of the room. 'You must've made a mistake!' Donovan glared at Matt.

'Not at all. Your wife is well advanced in her pregnancy, Mr Kilerne,' Matt replied at once.

Gwyneth burst into tears. Matt looked down at her. 'Now, where are these pains?'

Donovan shuffled back to join them and Abbie saw that he was trying to recover from what must have been great embarrassment for him, as well as a profound shock. She also noted that during Matt's brief palpation of his patient's stomach there had been no sign of pain. It was clear that Gwyneth's biggest problem had been in breaking the news of the pregnancy to her husband.

'I'd say it was a slight tummy upset, which seems to be resolved now,' Matt said tactfully and Gwyneth nodded, looking relieved. 'Do you know when your last period was?'

Gwyneth shook her head.

'Well, in that case, I need to examine you properly,' he explained. Glancing at Abbie, he added, 'Either myself or Dr Ashby.'

'You'll do,' said Gwyneth. 'We'll go to the bedroom.' She emerged from her swathe of bedclothes, wrapped herself in an old plaid dressing-gown and trotted down a gloomy corridor. Matt followed, casting a rueful grin back at Abbie.

In their absence, Abbie warmed herself at the stove. Donovan disappeared and only the collie made her feel welcome as he padded across the floor and lay at her feet.

She wondered if her father had met with a similar response from the strange couple on that freezing winter's

night when he had come here with Sean to discover that
Gwyneth was miscarrying.

Bob Burchfield had taken all his patients' troubles to
heart. He had disobeyed every rule in medicine in doing
so, but that was the kind of man he had been. He would
have worried bitterly over Gwyneth, Abbie reflected sadly.

After a while, she stood up and wandered around the
room. Why had Gwyneth not told Donovan she was expecting again? Did she fear another miscarriage? Was
Donovan opposed to having any more children? There were
any number of reasons, she supposed, but one thing was
certain, and that was that Gwyneth had manufactured the
stomach pains as a cry for help with the pregnancy.

Eventually Matt returned, giving her a mischievous wink.
'I would estimate, roughly, eighteen to twenty weeks,' he
said as he occupied a chair and wrote on Gwyneth's notes.
'The scan will tell us accurately.'

'Don't want no scan,' objected Donovan as his wife returned to the room.

'Why?' asked Matt, frowning.

'Don't believe in 'em,' said Donovan shortly.

'So you don't want your baby to have the best treatment
possible?' Matt shrugged. 'You're willing to take the risk
and deliver the baby yourself at an unknown date?'

'Deliver sheep,' he replied bluntly and for a moment
Abbie saw Matt's face tighten.

'Have you ever lost any lambs, Mr Kilerne?' Matt's dark
eyes glinted.

'Can't afford to lose 'em,' barked the truculent man.

'Then you'll agree that a human baby is far more delicate
in its development than a sheep,' Matt retorted swiftly.

Donovan's face darkened. 'I should know. Lost one already, thanks to you lot.'

'Your wife had a miscarriage,' Matt said, looking the
man steadily in the eye. 'It happens sometimes and there

is nothing that anyone can do about it. Many people resolve their grief by accepting that nature has intervened for a reason we shall never know, but have to trust that, indeed, nature reflected what was best for all.'

The room was silent as Matt rose and returned the notes to his case. When he had finished closing it, he looked at Gwyneth. 'It's important for you to have regular checks, which include a scan,' he told her firmly. 'You are your baby's life support machine. The baby is dependent on you for survival. Now, I shall expect to see you in surgery after you've attended the hospital appointment.'

The candid observation clearly startled the woman and she looked from Matt to her husband. There was a moment of indecision but finally she nodded.

'The truck's broke,' objected her husband.

'Will it be roadworthy soon?' Matt asked.

'Might be,' said Donovan with a shrug.

'I'll take that as a yes,' Matt said shortly, eyeing the man with dark, warning eyes.

'No need to be fussin',' Donovan agreed. 'It'll be done all right.'

'I'll keep you to your word, Mr Kilerne.' Matt stood up, glancing around the room. 'I take it you're not on the phone?'

'Don't believe in 'em.' Donovan shrugged.

Matt frowned. 'Where did you phone from today?'

'Neighbour down the hill.'

'We have their number at the surgery,' Abbie said, remembering that her father had managed to contact the Kilernes by this method. 'It hasn't changed, has it, Mr Kilerne?'

'Not as far as I knows, it 'asn't.' Donovan crossed the room and opened the wooden door. There were no thanks for their visit as they departed.

In the car, Matt shook his head as he turned on the wipers. 'That was quite a welcome,' he commented dryly.

'It seemed he still blames Dad for the miscarriage,' Abbie sighed as she buckled her belt.

'I'm not so sure.' He shrugged as he turned the key in the starter. 'I think that man is carrying a personal burden.'

'What makes you say that?' Abbie asked, frowning.

'Well, as a farmer it's obvious he has learned to accept mortality among his animals,' remarked Matt, as the powerful beam of the headlights lit up the wet gravel in front of them, 'but he couldn't when it came to his own child. I think there is probably something we don't know about going on in the depths of Mr Kilerne's troubled mind.'

Abbie didn't know what to think but, grateful that Matt had been there to support her, she reached across and laid her hand on his arm. 'Matt… It was much easier tonight, coming here. Thank you.'

In answer he smiled and bent across to kiss her. Then, revving the powerful Citroën engine, he reversed back along the lane and they began the journey home.

CHAPTER NINE

THE journey home was hair-raising. Wind drove furiously across the Cumbrian hills and shook the Citröen as though it were a toy. Had it not been for Matt's calm concentration and firm hold on the car, the journey might have been a nightmare, Abbie thought as she gripped the edge of her seat.

Matt carefully negotiated the first hairpin bend and the headlights illuminated the steep descent ahead of them.

It was easy to see how a car could skid out of control on black ice, Abbie thought sadly as she gazed out onto the road. Their path was tricky enough normally, but in freezing conditions it was no wonder the wheels of Sean's car had skidded over the skating rink of a road. The plunge through the insubstantial fence would have been unavoidable when the wheels had failed to grip the impossible surface.

'Not long now,' Matt said beside her. She nodded as the noise of the wind suddenly seemed to abate, Eventually they made it to the smooth flat road of the valley beneath.

Much later they reached a deserted Rendale and Matt took the road toward his cottage. Once inside, Abbie showered and wrapped herself in a warm towelling robe while Matt raided the fridge and concocted a stir-fry and cold chicken. Far too ravenous to bother setting the table, they ferried their plates into the small front room and ate from trays balanced on their knees.

After supper they attempted to discuss the Kilernes' problems, but it was clear they were both exhausted. 'Let's go to bed,' Matt said eventually. 'You look all in.'

Abbie nodded. 'I am a bit. What about you?'

Placing their empty plates to one side, he pulled her up from the sofa. 'I think I'll make it upstairs—as long as I have you lying beside me when I get there.' She reached up and slid her hands around his neck, covering his lips with her mouth in a deep, lingering kiss. 'Thank you for today,' she whispered.

He gave a small groan as he returned her kiss. 'Turn off the light,' he whispered, 'and let's go to bed. Though, at this rate, I could almost suggest we lie down on the sofa again.'

'Tempting,' she mused, fighting the tiredness and stifling a yawn. 'But the thought of that huge bed upstairs…'

He laughed softly and, despite the bone-weary tiredness he must have been feeling, he lifted her into his arms as though she were weightless, pulled her against his chest and carried her upstairs to bed.

Abbie's head rested in the crook of Matt's arm, her shoulder curved to his chest, her hand lying lightly on the inky pool of crisp, night-black hair that covered his chest. How long, she wondered, could she lie here and marvel at the texture of his skin, tawny and smooth, the faintest drift of aftershave rising from it?

She moved slightly, intent on her subject. She wanted to drink him in from every angle, overdose on the high cheekbones, the ebony lashes, the long, aquiline nose. Was there the faintest bump at the bridge? Were his ears just visible under the ruffled cap of thick, dark hair?

As if her frantic, noisy thoughts had called out to him, he awoke, stretched and smiled—the lazy, intimate smile that had the power to drive any other irrelevant thought from her mind.

'What,' he murmured, drawing her against him, 'are you thinking?'

She smiled, for how could she tell him? Where would she start?

'No regrets?' he asked suddenly, his brow creasing. Transformed, his face was a study of alarm, but she smiled.

'No regrets, none at all.'

His face cleared, feature by feature settling into repose once more. 'And so what are you thinking?'

She gazed into the sleepy, concerned eyes, wondering how it was possible to feel you had known someone for a lifetime when you had only known them for one summer. 'Cause,' she murmured lazily, 'and effect.'

'Ah,' he sighed. 'Interesting…'

'You and I meeting by chance. The first time I saw you at Joely's and wondered why you were there.'

He moved his position beside her, resting his head close to her face and smoothing her dark hair on the pillow as he gazed into her eyes. 'I knew when I saw you that you were the reason I had come to England. It was something deep down inside. A gut reaction. Almost as though I knew you, which, of course, I didn't.'

She looked at him uncertainly. 'Do you mean that?'

'Maybe it was fate,' he said softly. 'Do you believe in it, Abbie? Do you believe that some people are meant to meet by accident?'

She was not sure what she believed in these days. Matt had turned all logical reasoning on its head. No doubt if he had not so successfully occupied her mind over the past few hours she would have been unable to wrench her thoughts away from what had happened up there on Esk Fell. Instead, here she was, lying beside him, feeling as though her body were hovering on a fluffy white cloud.

She gazed into the sleepy brown eyes flecked with a glittering amber. A warm glow spread through her limbs as she thought of their love-making. Now, in the early

hours of the morning, she wanted nothing more but to remain here, feeling the way she did.

With a pang of sadness she recalled Sean's withdrawn
and mechanical responses, which had left her feeling unfulfilled and lonely. She had never really admitted failure
to herself. It had been easier to believe the fault was hers.

But before his death they had begun to quarrel, her body
craving the baby and motherhood that she had yearned for
so long. Their arguments had deepened into protracted and
depressing silences, widening the chasm between them.

She had known in her heart that they were growing apart
and that children would not have resolved their problems.
Eventually she had dropped the subject completely.

'I don't know the answer to that,' she whispered as she
turned into his arms, suddenly not wanting to think about
the past or the pain associated with it. 'But I'm willing to
be convinced.'

He pulled her against him, smoothing his hands along
her thighs and over the narrow dip of her waist, his fingers
coming up to follow a path over the softness of her breast.
Bringing his arms around her and kissing her again until
she was breathless, he drew a groan from her throat as she
ached with a growing desire that left her yearning for more,
her body trembling in his arms.

Along with the gales that had caused havoc over the weekend, there was an outbreak of summer flu. The next fort-
night saw many such casualties fill the surgery, residents
and holiday-makers alike running temperatures and com-
plaining of nausea.

Cottages in the valley were flood-damaged and the inevitable mopping-up process began. Sickness and diarrhoea
were a persistent complaint, many people blaming the
warm but wet conditions of the unpredictable summer.

Along with the flu virus, the crisis caused Matt's TR

surgery to swell. Residents and tourists alike demanded swift attention, and Abbie found herself adding another hour to her already overlong day.

One Friday afternoon in August Abbie arrived at the surgery and saw Marion Foster, her son Jonathan and, most surprising of all, Gwyneth Kilerne, all sitting in the waiting room.

'Hello, Dr Ashby,' Marion greeted her as she rose and walked over. 'I'm going to Dr Carrig's clinic with Jonathan.' She gestured to the three-year-old boy beside her, who gave Abbie a huge smile, revealing a large gap between his front teeth. 'He's had that flu bug and I want to make sure he's all right.'

At that point Jonathan's name was called and, taking her son's hand, Marion said goodbye and bustled off towards the corridor.

Abbie turned and met Gwyneth's sombre gaze, a noticeable contrast to that of Jonathan's. 'Hello, Gwyneth,' she said. 'How are you?'

'Don't know,' said Gwyneth glumly. 'That's why I come to see you.'

'Me?' Abbie was more than surprised that Gwyneth was not booked to see Matt who, on the Esk Fell trip, had appeared to win her confidence.

'Can't stop long,' said Gwyneth with predictable abruptness. 'Made sure I got the first appointment.'

'In that case, you'd better come along,' Abbie replied, and led the way back to her consulting room, still mystified as to why Gwyneth hadn't booked an appointment with Matt.

Gwyneth nervously took the patient's chair, her long skirt and woolly jumper disguising the pregnancy she had been at such pains to hide from her husband.

Abbie took the records that were on the top of the pile and, checking that they were Gwyneth's, drew out the report which had arrived in the office earlier that week. Matt had shown it to Abbie and they had discussed the problem of persuading Gwyneth to have a hospital delivery, an arrangement they both knew she and Donovan would resist.

'The scan was satisfactory, Gwyneth,' Abbie said as she indicated the report. 'I'm sure you must be relieved to know all is well.'

'S'pose so,' Gwyneth acknowledged grudgingly. 'Those scans don't tell you everything, though, do they?'

'Not everything, but enough for us to detect, for instance, a multiple birth.'

'Twins don't run in the family,' said Gwyneth. 'I could have told you that.'

Abbie let the remark pass as she folded the rubber cuff around her patient's arm in order to take her blood pressure. 'Are you getting enough rest?' she enquired, remembering Gwyneth's last fall on the hillside which had preceded her miscarriage.

'I still look after some of the animals,' Gwyneth mumbled. 'But not the sheep.'

'What animals do you keep, other than the sheep?' Abbie asked as she wrote Gwyneth's satisfactory reading in her notes.

'Goats and a few chickens,' Gwyneth replied, tugging down her woolly sleeve. 'We have goat's milk, cheese and eggs and chicken in the freezer.'

'No doubt you grow your own vegetables?' Abbie persevered trying to expand the conversation.

'Course!' Gwyneth exclaimed sharply, as though Abbie was stating the obvious. 'Don't spray them neither. Everything we eats is natural.'

Abbie looked down at her notes, feeling duly admonished. Eventually she frowned. 'I would feel happier if you had a telephone, Gwyneth. I suppose there's no chance you could have one installed?'

'Donovan don't like phones,' snapped Gwyneth. 'Won't have one at the cottage.'

'I see.' Abbie paused. 'Have you given any thought to where you'll have the baby?' she asked quietly.

'At home,' Gwyneth replied. 'Donovan don't like hospitals.'

'No, I'm aware of that, but in view of your medical history—' Abbie began, only to be interrupted.

'Won't go amiss again this time,' Gwyneth said, her voice shaky. 'Not with this one.'

'I'm pleased to hear that,' Abbie said hesitantly, wondering if Gwyneth was acknowledging the miscarriage being a result of her fall and not because of her father's or Sean's negligence. 'Even so, will you and Donovan please think about what I have said?' she persisted.

Gwyneth shrugged. 'Donovan has no time for you lot.'

'Well, I'm sorry to hear that.' With a dart of disappointment, Abbie decided she *had* misunderstood Gwyneth's meaning. 'All right,' she sighed. 'If you'd like to pop up on the scales, we'll take your weight.'

When Abbie had completed Gwyneth's first antenatal appointment, she helped her patient on with her cardigan and walked with her to the door. 'Did your husband drive you here this morning?' she asked curiously.

Gwyneth nodded. 'Won't come in. He's waiting outside in the truck.'

'And you will be sure to come in for next month's appointment?' Abbie asked again.

'He says he'll bring me.' Gwyneth looked at Abbie under her dark eyelashes. 'Didn't want this baby, he didn't. Said after the accident happened it would bring bad luck.'

'Do you believe in this—bad luck, Gwyneth?' Abbie asked.

Gwyneth was silent. Then she said, 'That's why I didn't

tell him about the baby. Bad luck, you see. And then when you turned up on the doorstep…'

'You thought that I was more of this bad luck?' Abbie guessed.

Gwyneth dropped her head.

'Well, I don't know if this helps,' Abbie replied levelly, 'but for what it's worth, I'm certain your bad luck is in the past. I think this baby will grow up to be fit and healthy. I hope you believe that, too.'

Gwyneth didn't reply, but again she looked up from under the curtain of wild hair. 'What hospital would it be— if I decided?' she asked suddenly.

'We could arrange for the delivery at Rendale Cottage—'

'I'll think about it,' Gwyneth muttered. Gathering her cardigan around her, she promptly departed.

It was only after Gwyneth had left that Abbie realised that luck—bad luck, in particular—obviously played a major part in the Kilernes' lives. With Donovan's pessimistic attitude, in particular his aversion to all things medical, the fact that she had managed to persuade Gwyneth to think about a hospital delivery was a milestone in itself.

After surgery she returned her files to the office. Matt was there, sliding his own patient records back into the carousel. He looked up and smiled. 'I've something rather unusual to tell you,' he said as he pushed back his hair with his palm, as though he, too, found the news bewildering. 'It's about Jasper.'

She tensed, expecting bad news. 'What is it, Matt?'

A faint smile crossed his lips. 'I told Jasper about Dave Carter, thinking Jasper might have one or two connections in the Lakes. But our conversation took another turn altogether. Jasper offered Dave and Marion the flat attached to his house. It's been empty for about fifteen years, since his mother died. He said the rent would be minimal in return for a small amount of gardening and odd jobs.'

'Have you told them yet?' asked Abbie in surprise.

'Yes. I rang Dave Carter who said the activity centre have given him a desk job. After work tonight he and Marion are going to see the flat.'

'And Marion has had some nursing experience,' Abbie said thoughtfully. 'Does Jasper know they are expecting a child?'

'Jasper said as long as they keep themselves to themselves, he'll be satisfied.' Matt grinned. 'He did remark that perhaps if he had someone living in the same house everyone would stop pestering him.'

Abbie raised her eyebrows. 'Meaning Jackie, I suppose.'

Matt didn't reply, but as they set about the rest of the morning Abbie reflected that Jasper and Matt had discussed more between them than Matt had revealed and that Matt had probably edited much of what Jasper had really said.

One balmy late August morning the sun burst through the cloud and shone so defiantly that even the tarmac looked as if it was melting.

Matt's children's clinic had become very popular, and the children he had begun with were slowly discharged and replaced by others. Little Monica Kay's leg gradually straightened and Katey lost her unsightly puppy fat with the help of *Katey in The Kitchen*. Even Janine Gillette's ear infections cleared eventually.

The amount of time Abbie spent at home grew less as she invariably returned to the cottage of an evening and Don and Bonnie continued to be totally absorbed in Blotters. Phil and Joely became skilled hosts of summer barbecues, Michele suffered no further bouts of tonsillitis and even the Kilernes' attitude mellowed. The conversation Abbie had had with Gwyneth meant that their next meeting was easier, and Gwyneth seemed to be relieved that her baby, due in November, was to be delivered in Rendale Cottage hospital.

September seemed to catch everyone unawares. The Indian summer brought more visitors than ever to view the beauty of the Cumbrian landscape. But there was one continuing sadness for Abbie. Jasper Macdonald's health deteriorated quickly. The arrangement with Marion and Dave, however, worked better than Abbie had dared to hope.

On a warm evening, on the way back from the surgery to the cottage, she decided to pay him a visit. Her calls were always brief and she had learned to accept the inevitable progression of his disease, doing what she could for him in the way of pain relief.

The last time she had visited, two weeks before, Marion had opened the front door and welcomed her. An unspoken agreement seemed to have been reached between Jasper and his lodgers. Marion would answer the door and the telephone and had taken to doing a little light housework. Jasper still fed and bathed himself. It helped him to maintain a semblance of normality and, unlike Jackie, Marion refused to treat Jasper like an invalid.

Abbie stopped the car outside Jasper's house. The garden, always a concern to Jasper, now looked orderly. Even the Russian vine had been trimmed and no longer obscured the porch. Abbie knew it was Dave's handiwork and that over the past weeks, after returning each evening from a desk job he had been given at the activity centre, he had quietly begun to restore the old house, grateful for the opportunity to compensate Jasper for their low rent.

Abbie locked her car and walked up to the big front door. She was about to knock when she noticed the bright red glow of a new bell-push. She pressed it and listened to the chime of the bell inside the hall.

Marion answered the door. 'Hello, Dr Ashby,' she said. 'Come in.'

'How are you?' Abbie asked.

Marion nodded. 'I feel fine, thanks.'

'And Jasper?'

'Not too good,' Marion answered in a soft voice. She signalled and Abbie followed her into the kitchen. 'He's resting in the front room. We made up the bed-settee for him last night. I'm afraid, even with our help, he can't manage the stairs any more.'

'Oh, dear,' Abbie sighed. 'How are you coping?'

'Oh, Mr Macdonald never complains,' Marion said at once. 'But I know for a fact that the nights are bad for him.' She lifted a large blue Thermos from the worktop and began to screw down the top. 'I'm often up with backache myself. Once or twice I've knocked because I've noticed his hall light on. You can just see the shaft of light under the connecting door. When the light is off I know he's asleep.'

'And he answers your knock?' Abbie asked in surprise.

Marion nodded. 'Oh, yes. He seems pleased to have company. I've taken to reading to him. That seems to settle him a bit.'

Abbie smiled. 'You're very kind, Marion.'

'It's us who are the grateful ones,' Marion answered quickly. 'The flat has given us time to look for somewhere permanent.' She paused. 'Dave is back at the activity centre, working in the office. It's less money, but we're managing.'

'And Jonathan?'

'He's very happy here. I can't believe how lucky we are.' She bit her lip. 'I don't know what would have happened to us if Mr Macdonald hadn't helped.'

Abbie smiled. 'Well, I'm pleased it's worked out well. I'd better go in now.'

'Will you take the Thermos along? It's hot tea for him to drink during the evening. It saves him having to struggle to the kitchen.'

Abbie followed Marion through to the hall, where she slipped through the connecting door and back into her own part of the house. Abbie made her way to the front room and tapped on the door.

'Come in.' Jasper lay on the bed-settee, a blanket draped over his legs.

'Hello, Jasper.' She smiled but it was difficult to act normally as his drastic weight loss had reduced his features to bone. She placed the Thermos on the table beside him. He made a pretence of scowling, but accepted the Thermos with what Abbie felt was a look of appreciation.

'Sit down,' he told her gruffly. 'I hope you're not here to try to persuade me I'm dying.'

Abbie laughed and he also chuckled.

'Thought you might be that old witch of a nurse,' he grumbled.

'But Jackie hasn't called on you for several months,' said Abbie as she took a seat. 'Since before you let out the flat.'

'She only wanted me to go into an institution!'

'A hospice,' Abbie corrected gently.

'Well, I'm staying put.' He looked at her archly. 'Anyway, I've company now. No one need poke their noses in.'

'I have to admit that was a very ingenious idea of yours,' agreed Abbie with a rueful smile. 'Now, let's have a listen to that chest of yours.' She took out her stethoscope and leaned forward. Pushing back his pyjama jacket, she tried to hide her dismay at his thin neck and emaciated chest. However, what she feared most, the onset of a respiratory infection, did not appear to be in evidence.

'Has the physiotherapist called this week?' she asked.

Jasper shrugged. 'No. Doesn't need to. The girl does it.'

'You mean Marion helps you?'

'Does a better job, too.'

Abbie folded away her stethoscope. 'I take it the arrangement is working, then?'

'Fairish,' he acknowledged vaguely. After a few seconds of coughing he slipped back on the pillows. 'And what about you, girl?'

'Oh, I'm fine.' Abbie shrugged.

'And the man himself?' he prompted, arching a shaggy grey eyebrow.

'If you mean Matt…' Abbie smiled ruefully '…you see enough of him to know exactly how he is.'

'Fine fellow,' Jasper said with a grin. 'Good doctor. All you'd need in a good partner.'

Abbie shook her head and said slowly, 'You know the situation, Jasper.'

'I was thinking—'

'I know what you were thinking,' Abbie interrupted. 'Now, I'm here to talk about you. Not me.'

'Who says so?'

'Do you ever give in?'

'When people fall in love, things change,' he murmured.

'Who said anything about love?' Abbie shifted her attention to her case and reached out to lock it.

'It's there in your eyes, young woman.' He coughed again, so painfully this time that Abbie had to assist him, supporting him as he tried to sit up. Finally he sank back on the pillows.

'And all this about love from a committed bachelor,' she joked as she drew up the blanket.

'Yes, but I've studied people all my life.' He caught hold of her wrist with shaky hands. 'You know people by their eyes. The hills…you come to know by climbing them.' His voice trailed off as his eyelids fluttered. 'This disease is the biggest hill I've had to climb… I've realised I need folk to help me on the way. Marion and her man—they're good people. They love each other. And they still have time for a sick old man.'

Abbie covered his hand with her own. 'Try to rest now, Jasper.'

'You need someone to love, too, girl,' he whispered before he closed his eyes.

She remained with him until he fell asleep, then, brushing away the dampness at the corners of her eyes, she rose and quietly left the room.

At the front door the fading summer and all its beauty rushed to greet her—scents of flowers, mown grass, crispy leaves, breathtaking colours. Some precious part of this beauty had touched Jasper. If his illness had disabled him physically, his spirit seemed renewed.

As she walked to the car, she recalled his comment about needing someone to love. It consoled her to know that he had found people to care about and people who cared about him.

And when, a few seconds later, she glanced into her driving mirror she saw the truth of Jasper's observations. What he had seen in her eyes was love. Love that would remain with her, in some measure, for the rest of her life.

CHAPTER TEN

'WE WON,' said Arthur Haskins as he lowered himself into the chair. 'We actually won.'

Abbie smiled as she sat down behind her desk. 'Congratulations, Arthur.'

'And we were bottom of the league, that's what I can't understand.' Arthur shook his head disbelievingly. 'We put the Hobcraig first division to shame. Honestly, they were crying into their beer.' He laughed and winked. 'Well, almost.'

'You obviously played well,' Abbie replied.

Arthur went red. 'I have to admit, I did. That is, we all did. But I felt as if I had magic in my fingers.'

'You're still not smoking?'

Arthur shook his head. 'It's four months now.'

'And you've only had one serious angina attack in all that time?'

'That's amazing, too,' replied Arthur. 'I mean, I was having them so frequently. It must have been the cigars, I suppose. I never thought I'd hear myself say that, but it's true.'

'Your blood pressure is much lower,' Abbie said as she folded away the rubber cuff of the sphygmomanometer. 'And your chest is also clear. Well done.'

'It's all down to that young man of yours,' Arthur said as he rolled down his sleeve. 'He made me realise life wasn't over for me. OK, so I'm in my seventies, but I've two decades of living ahead of me—if I try. Just think how many matches we could win in that time.'

Abbie smiled. 'It's nice to hear you talking so positively,

147

Arthur. Obviously you're determined not to smoke again…'

'No way!' Arthur beamed at her. 'It's never too late to stop. And now I've stopped, it's like a curtain's been lifted from my eyes. I can see again. Life is rich. It's like the story of that Aborigine. I know exactly how he felt.'

Suddenly there was a knock on the door. Abbie looked up and called, 'Come in.'

Matt pushed open the door. 'Sorry to interrupt. I'm just shooting out and I wanted a word with Arthur before I left.'

She nodded. 'Go ahead. We've just finished.'

'Hello, Dr Carrig.' Arthur stood up. 'I was hoping I might see you, too.'

'I understand congratulations are in order,' Matt said with a grin. 'Top of the league table, I hear?'

'How did you know?' Arthur frowned.

'Elspeth called in for her yearly check with the practice nurse. I happened to see her and she gave me the news.'

Again, Arthur reddened. 'I don't know what to say, Dr Carrig, except thank you.'

'Don't thank me,' Matt shrugged. 'It took a lot of will-power to do what you did. Hence…' Matt dug in his pocket and pulled out a small package. 'Just something to remember me by.'

Arthur accepted the gift and looked in embarrassment at both Abbie and Matt. 'I'm lost for words,' he muttered.

Matt grinned. 'Well, I must be on my way. Er…sorry to interrupt, Dr Ashby.'

Abbie smiled, her colour deepening. 'Not at all, Dr Carrig.'

'See you, Arthur. And keep up the good work.'

Matt met Abbie's eyes before he quietly closed the door. She felt the familiar flutter of her heart and then, as she turned her attention back to Arthur, she was amused to see that he was unwrapping his parcel.

'It's a set of darts!' Arthur exclaimed. 'With my initials "A.R." inscribed on the flights.' He showed them to Abbie, removing one of the darts from its anchor and holding it up to the light.

'They're beautiful,' said Abbie in genuine surprise.

'I've never had such a lovely set,' Arthur said, his voice husky. Then he frowned at Abbie. 'What did he mean, to remember him by?'

Abbie's face clouded. 'Didn't you know? Dr Carrig is returning to Australia.'

Arthur looked shocked. 'I suppose I must have forgotten that. Dr Carrig just seems like you or Dr Morgan—a piece of the furniture now. When does he leave?'

Abbie said, 'In October.'

'But that's next month!' Arthur protested as he lay the dart back in the box.

'I'm afraid so.'

'Well,' said Arthur with a sigh as he slipped the box in his trouser pocket, 'I'm certainly sorry to hear it.'

'Yes,' agreed Abbie. 'We are, too. However, Dr Morgan and I have decided to replace Dr Carrig with a third member of staff. A permanent partner. So it isn't all bad news for our patients.'

Arthur lifted his shoulders. 'But there won't be many to match him, that's for sure.' He walked to the door and stood there, rubbing his chin. 'Anyway, thanks a lot, Dr Carrig. I hope I don't see you too soon,' he joked. Raising his hand in salute, he went on his way.

Abbie realised she was sitting stiffly in her chair, gripping the pen so fiercely her knuckles were white. She dropped it onto her blotter and deliberately sat back against the cool leather. She took a deep breath and closed her eyes, denying the ache in her heart that the conversation with Arthur had precipitated. She thought if she managed to deny it long enough, the pain would go away. But, if any-thing, it deepened.

Matt was leaving and yet it seemed she hadn't fully ac-cepted the fact yet. Spring and summer had flown. It seemed in some way as if her whole life had been encom-passed in those months, making it difficult to remember what had happened before. Even yesterday, when Frank had suggested it was time to advertise for a new partner, she had agreed mechanically. But today she had heard those words, ''something to remember me by'', and suddenly it seemed that Matt's leaving was real.

She knew he would try to avoid hurting her. Had today's casual mention been for her benefit as well as Arthur's? Matt need not have come into the room. He could have left Arthur's gift at the desk with Rachel. Was this his way of gently reminding her?

Abbie rose and made her way out to Reception. Arthur had disappeared and the waiting room was empty.

'Are you going out to lunch?' Rachel asked as Abbie lowered her head over the appointment book.

'I think I'll have a snack here,' she replied.

'In that case, would you like to look over this and give me your comments?' Rachel handed her a sheet of A4 pa-per enclosed in a Cellophane wallet. 'Dr Morgan sketched out a few ideas.'

Abbie frowned as she studied the clear, bold handwrit-ing. Clearly, Frank was as eager as Abbie had been in the spring to look for a permanent replacement. Only now it was Abbie who was having difficulty in adjusting to the prospect.

The words swam in front of her eyes. Arthur Haskins had been right when he had remarked that it would be difficult to find someone to equal Matt at the surgery.

'I'll give it some thought,' Abbie said as she looked up at Rachel who was frowning at her.

'Dr Morgan said if you'd like to add your ideas and then go ahead and put the advertisement in the journal, he'd leave it to you. He also said in view of the time factor...' Rachel shrugged. 'This summer has just flown, hasn't it?'

Abbie nodded. 'Yes, it has.' She added the wallet to her correspondence and tried to avoid catching Rachel's curious stare. None of the receptionists or Jill or the nurses had commented on her relationship with Matt, yet their affair must now be obvious to one and all.

Her head down, she fled to the staffroom. When she finally found herself alone, she took a breath and steadied herself against the back of a chair. It was ridiculous, she told herself, behaving like this. For goodness sake, she had known all along that Matt was leaving.

Trying to clear her head, she felt an unpleasant swimming sensation in her stomach. The feeling gripped her for a moment and, sitting down, she leaned forward, taking her time to breathe deeply. The nausea persisted, as it had done occasionally lately, and it was some time before she relaxed and felt better.

She would have to get a grip of herself, she realised. Fainting fits during working hours were not welcome. As the nausea receded, she relaxed back in her chair, reflecting that flu was the last thing she needed at the moment. With a redoubled effort she rose, made herself a cup of strong, sugared tea and drank it without any pleasure at all.

'Aunt Abbie, look what I've got!' Michele ran down the garden path, her blonde plaits bouncing on her shoulders.

Abbie stopped as her niece hurtled towards her. 'Hi, mischief. Oh, look what we have here. Lots of red and green paper,' Abbie said with a serious expression. 'And string all muddled up in the middle of it.'

Breathless, Michele stared up at her aunt. 'It's a kite, silly!' she cried, giggling. 'It's got be ass-assel—'

'Assembled?' said Abbie, laughing.

'You knew!' Michele exclaimed, peals of laughter drifting back to the cottage. 'Uncle Phil bought it for us to fly this afternoon. We're going up to Windy Ridge.'

For a child not yet five years of age Michele was as bright as a button. Abbie felt proud of her niece as they walked towards the cottage. Michele chattered away, her conversation clear and defined, never at a loss for words. She tried hard to experiment with new vocabulary and she loved to read. Perhaps Michele would be one of those fortunate children who…

Abbie stopped herself, realising that her thoughts concerning Michele were racing ahead. Her maternal instincts seemed to have surfaced lately. All week she had been trying to handle feelings of one sort of another. Michele had filled that empty space inside her, the ache which had been compounded with Matt's presence in her life.

Almost in the same instant as she thought of this she looked up into the bespectacled face of Phil Sheppey. 'Hi, Phil,' she said, and flushed slightly. 'I hope that kite is easier to build than it looks.'

Phil grinned. He took the kite that Michele pushed into his hands and rolled his eyes. 'I don't know what I've let myself in for now.'

'You *do* know!' exclaimed Michele, wide-eyed. 'Else you wouldn't have bought it for me.'

Phil pulled at the strings. 'Let's see what we can do. I seem to remember this bit goes through here…'

Michele slipped her hand into Phil's and led him off into the front room. 'See you later, Aunt Abbie.'

'Bye, darling.' Abbie stood there, watching Michele and Phil disappear into the garden. She had fully expected Michele to be at a loose end, her dancing class postponed this Saturday due to the teacher's annual holiday. Abbie had intended to take Michele to the matinée performance of *One Hundred and One Dalmatians*, showing at the local cinema, so with several hours ahead of her Abbie found herself for once at a loose end.

Just as she was about to leave, Joely's voice came from the kitchen. 'I'm in here, Abbie. Making up a picnic!'

Abbie hesitated, then walked towards the kitchen. Joely was standing at the worktop, dressed in jeans and T-shirt, a baseball cap turned backwards on her blonde head.

'Just the person I wanted to see,' she said as she rolled a chicken drumstick into a strip of foil.

'Something smells delicious,' Abbie commented, occupying a stool at the breakfast bar.

'Oh, that's the spiced apple sponge cake.' Joely turned back to the oven. She slid on an oven glove and drew out a golden-coloured creation that caused Abbie to widen her eyes in admiration.

'Joe, that's spectacular!'

'It will be if it's edible.' Joely slid a knife through its centre. The blade came out cleanly. She raised her eyebrows. 'Not bad for a novice.'

Abbie giggled. 'It's the first cake I've ever seen you cook.'

Joely made a face. 'You're as bad as Michele is. You can't keep a secret, either of you. Here's me telling Phil I'll be the next Delia Smith!'

It was then, as Joely folded the greaseproof paper from the sponge, that Abbie caught the delicate sparkle on her sister's finger. For a second it vanished and Abbie thought she must have been mistaken. However, as Joely removed the paper covering, disposed of it and returned the cake to a wire tray, the ring glinted again.

Abbie looked up into her sister's face. 'Joe—what's that?'

Joely followed Abbie's gaze. She lifted her hand and

held it out towards Abbie, wiggling her finger. 'Do you like it?'

Abbie nodded as the single solitaire sparkled in the light. 'It's beautiful, Joe.'

'It's a diamond,' her sister said and blushed. 'Phil popped the question.'

'You mean, you two are engaged?'

Joely nodded. 'Are you surprised?'

Abbie stared at her sister, then slowly shook her head. 'No, Joe, not really. Are you sure it's what you want?''

Her sister perched beside her on a stool. 'Oh, yes. I love him very much. And he says he loves us both—that's all I needed to know before I said yes. I haven't told Michele yet. Or Mum. You're the first.'

Abbie leaned forward to hug her sister. 'I don't think either of them will be surprised. Congratulations, Joe.'

'I think he'll make a good father for Michele,' her sister said as she drew away. 'Otherwise, of course, I wouldn't have considered marriage. He's getting a desk job with the paper which means he won't be away so much.'

'Where are you going to live?' Abbie asked after a few moments.

'Here, for a while,' her sister told her. 'That way it won't be too much of a change for Michele. Of course, we'll need a bigger place later on, but by then we'll all be ready to move as a family.'

Abbie nodded, reflecting that Joely seemed to have grown up in front of her eyes this summer. And she had made a good choice in Phil, Abbie was certain.

Joely looked at her suddenly. 'We wanted a Christmas wedding. Nothing big, a service at the registry office and a reception at one of the Lake hotels afterwards. We would like you and Matt as witnesses.'

Abbie looked down at the picnic hamper. 'Joe, that's sweet of you, but it's impossible.'

'Because Matt's leaving, you mean?'

Abbie nodded. 'I'm sorry.' She shrugged. 'Otherwise there would have been nothing better I would have liked to do.'

'Couldn't you persuade Matt to stay on longer?' Joely asked.

Abbie shook her head. 'He has a job to go back to. Australia is his home, Joe. I understood that from the start.'

Her sister looked disappointed. 'But you two seem so right together.'

At this Abbie fell silent. Then swiftly, before her sister could speak again, she said, 'Frank and I will be interviewing for a replacement during the first week of September.'

Joely sighed. 'I wish it were both of us. Wouldn't that be wonderful, Abs? Both of us getting married on the same day?'

It was a thought that almost broke Abbie's heart. A thought that seemed to pierce the very core of her being. A mental picture that, once given life in the mind, caused the sweetest, most bitter of pains.

'I'll let you finish your picnic,' Abbie said, and slipped off the stool, kissing her sister briefly on the cheek.

Then she fled.

During the second week of September, an e-mail arrived at Jill Nials's workstation in the office. The communication was from a Geraldine Hooley, written and sent from Dubai.

Matt caught up with Abbie before she left for her calls. 'From Jill,' he said as she paused in the waiting room and he handed her the paper. 'Looks like your first applicant.'

Abbie read the neat typeface. 'Yes, so it seems.'

'Are you going to answer it this evening?'

Abbie looked up into his face and saw the deep frown etched across his forehead that, she knew, indicated he was concerned for her sake. In the past two weeks neither of them had referred much to the arrangements Abbie had set about making for his replacement. They had exchanged a few brief comments, but that had been all. Now, it appeared, they must confront hard facts. 'I've a couple of calls to make first,' Abbie answered briskly, 'then I'll sit down and read it properly.'

Matt nodded. 'Have you had any other replies?'

'Not yet,' Abbie said, adding quickly, 'but I'm sure we will.'

He paused, as though about to say something, then gave a brief shrug. 'As I've no calls to make this evening, I'll make supper. What would you like?'

'You mean, I have a choice?' Abbie lifted wry eyebrows.

'Lasagne with salad, lasagne with rye bread,' he intoned. 'Or—'

'Or lasagne with fried potatoes?'

They laughed. The joke was that when Abbie had first opened Matt's freezer, a stack of frozen meals had toppled out. The majority of them were supermarket lasagne.

'Would it surprise you to know I had something else in mind?' he said looking mildly hurt.

'It would.' Abbie laughed. 'What is it?'

'Spaghetti Bolognese suit you, with lashings of sauce?'

'You're on. I'll stop for wine on the way home.'

'None of your cheap plonk,' Matt ordered. 'Let's have something special tonight. Something with a bit of zip.'

'Are we celebrating?' Abbie asked, moderating her voice as Rachel appeared behind the reception desk.

Before Abbie could move backwards, he bent to whisper, his lips grazing her cheek. 'We'll find something to celebrate,' he murmured, grinning. 'Don't be late.'

'Yes, Doctor.' Abbie smiled and hurried out into the warm September evening. Though she loved to drink a good wine with her meal occasionally, the thought of wine today held little attraction.

The unpleasant nausea that she had experienced a few weeks ago had persisted, though no flu had ensued. She had assumed that it would pass, given time, and had reasoned that her anxiety was the underlying problem.

Abbie tucked the e-mail into the pocket of her dress, intending to read it properly later. However, once in the car she paused, before starting the engine. She retrieved the paper from her pocket and began to read it.

Geraldine Hooley. A young doctor, with only one year of practical experience. Abbie hadn't thought about engaging someone as inexperienced as this, but Geraldine seemed eager and enthusiastic—must be to e-mail. She explained that her mother had seen the article in the journal and, knowing her daughter was searching for just such a post, had telephoned her in Dubai where she was on holiday.

Finally Abbie managed to put Geraldine out of her mind and drove to her first house call. Lyn Groves was in her thirties and when she answered the door to Abbie's knock she sneezed several times into a tissue. She wore a housecoat and slippers and sank breathlessly into a chair as soon as they entered the lounge.

Abbie examined her and, as she was doing so, noticed a half-full bottle of brandy on the coffee table.

'It's flu,' pronounced Abbie, 'so rest, paracetamol and plenty of fluids.'

'That's my remedy,' mumbled Lyn Groves, pointing to the alcohol. Her voice was slurred and she was having difficulty in focusing. Abbie had seen several cases of flu during the day, all having managed to travel into surgery for treatment.

In Lyn Groves's case, the problem had been the consumption of the brandy which had prevented her from driving, rather than the onset of flu. A fact that was close to irony, Abbie thought, recalling her earlier conversation with Matt and his suggestion of wine. Her own reaction had been to feel, as she was now, slightly nauseated at the mention of alcohol.

'Drink vitamin C,' Abbie advised. 'It's much better for you.'

'Can't you give me an antibiotic?' her patient asked, deciding to ignore Abbie's suggestion. 'I've got to be at work in the morning on an early shift.'

'Antibiotics have no effect on viruses.' Abbie gestured to the bottle. 'And brandy will only leave you with a hangover.'

'Well, there wasn't much use in me calling you out in that case,' said the woman rudely. It was a remark which Abbie felt deserved an answer, but she restrained herself from giving one as her patient was already distracted by the TV.

With a sigh, Abbie left and drove to her second call. This was an elderly man with almost the same symptoms as Lyn Groves. In his case, though, he was eager to accept advice and apologised for not having been able to travel in to the surgery.

It was, Abbie thought as she drove, the diversity of her work that was so fascinating, if sometimes frustrating. Most of the time people were only too pleased to take sensible medical advice, and general practice as a whole, apart from the exhausting night calls, was totally fulfilling.

The problem was, would a youngster like Geraldine Hooley adapt to such a challenge? An older doctor would know what to expect and would be able to deal with an unexpected crisis when it arose. Anyway, thought Abbie as she drove towards Matt's cottage, no use crossing bridges before you came to them. Perhaps, after supper this evening, she could talk to Matt about the problem.

It would be the first time she had actually sat down with him and discussed his departure. Feeling the knot of apprehension tighten in her stomach, she accelerated and headed for home.

After a delicious meal—with the wine she had bought on her way home, virtually untasted by either of them—Abbie helped Matt clear the table. Then, taking her hand, he led her out into the garden and pulled her down into the swing seat, the first coolness of September settling around them in a misty veil.

'It's chilly,' he said, sliding his arm around her. 'I think we've had the last of the good weather.'

Abbie snuggled against his chest. 'I could stay out here all night. Look at the stars. Hundreds of them.'

'I wonder what we look like to them.' Matt frowned. 'Whether we shine as brightly.' Abbie was lost in thought, staring at their radiance until Matt squeezed her arm. 'What are you thinking about?'

She sighed and shook her head. 'Only Geraldine Hooley. Wondering if she would adapt to Rendale.' Abbie leaned back against the seat and breathed in the crisp evening air, letting its coolness flow through her lungs. 'She's not had much experience, that's the biggest concern.'

'Nor had I when I came here,' he was swift to point out. 'At least not in general practice.'

'But you were thirty and you had specialised in paediatrics. Geraldine's in her early twenties, having had practically no experience at all.'

'If the love of medicine is there, if the attraction is a strong one, it doesn't matter. Geraldine Hooley might be destined for Rendale, just as I was. Otherwise I would never have met you.' He added softly, 'Which brings me to something I don't want to discuss, but we have to as you'll want to get my replacement arranged.'

Abbie pushed herself back, knowing what was about to come by the tone of his voice. Unsteadily, she met his gaze.

'I'm flying out on October the twenty eighth,' he told her. 'Phil's offered to drive me to Heathrow the night before.'

'I see,' Abbie said quietly, as for a moment everything spun around her. 'I would have driven you to London.'

He nodded. 'I think that would have been a bit too much for either of us to cope with, don't you?'

They fell into silence and, except for the creaking of the swing and the faint sound of a car passing, the evening silence deepened around them. After a while, he took hold of her hand. 'Abbie, is this what we both really want?'

She frowned. 'You mean, do I want you to go?' She shook her head. 'No, of course I don't. But it's hardly the point, Matt.'

'This doesn't have to be the end—' he began but she stopped him, shaking her head.

'Matt, we both know that saying that we would keep in contact just wouldn't work.' She sighed. 'We are going to be living on opposite sides of the world.'

'That wasn't exactly what I had in mind,' he said quietly. Then, as if he was about to say more, he leaned forward, lifted her hair from her face and tucked it behind her ear. 'Abbie, I'm not asking you to give anything up for me,' he continued, but before he could go on she interrupted him once more.

'I couldn't leave England, Matt, if that's what you were thinking,' she said, her voice husky. 'You have a career and family to go back to. My future is here in Rendale. We knew when we began this—'

Their eyes met and even in the darkness she could see the desire in his. She also knew that her own eyes were full of the same need. He reached across and pulled her into his arms. Her body trembled as he kissed her and her arms went tightly around his neck as she leaned against him. The next thing she knew they were climbing the stairs, leaving the autumn night and their unhappiness behind them.

CHAPTER ELEVEN

ABBIE sat in the conservatory of her family home and felt almost a stranger. Little clues of Don's presence were scattered about the house—a book on DIY, a coat hanging on the back of a door, the bathroom as pristine as always but with the addition of a bottle of men's cologne on the shelf.

She had been living at the cottage with Matt for so long now that the house seemed a lifetime away, and yet she would return to it…or would she? Could she?

Lately she had begun to think of looking for a home of her own. She had tried to find the enthusiasm to study some brochures or approach an agent. But it was no use. She found herself unable to concentrate, with Matt's departure so close at hand.

Her decision to take Geraldine Hooley onto the staff had been welcomed by Frank, and Geraldine had begun immediately.

'More tea, darling?' Bonnie asked as she came in with a freshly made pot of Earl Grey in her hands.

'Lovely.' Abbie watched her mother bend across to reach her cup. A waft of expensive perfume filtered her way. Abbie smiled reflectively. Her mother always looked perfectly groomed these days. And her conversation was as stimulating as her appearance. Thanks to a brisk season at Blotters, the shop had been a success.

'Phil and Joely are coming over later,' Bonnie said as she sat down. 'Sunday is the only time I have to make a family dinner. Will you stay and eat with us?'

Abbie shook her head. 'Thanks all the same, Mum. I'm cooking dinner this evening.'

162

Bonnie looked up. 'Is your new recruit enjoying her first week?'

Abbie sipped her tea, then nodded. 'We're in the process of transferring Matt's patients to Geraldine. She has a natural aptitude with children, so the children who have got used to seeing Matt on a Friday are continuing in the same way. Other than that, we've had no real problems.'

'So, despite your reservations on her age,' Bonnie said, lifting an eyebrow, 'she's settling in well?'

Abbie smiled. 'Despite reservations on age and experience, yes.'

'Which goes to show that age is really no barrier if the love is there.'

'Are we still talking about Geraldine?' Abbie guessed her mother was making a point, though she was surprised at what she said next.

'Don is almost twelve years older than me,' Bonnie said with a small shrug. 'He doesn't look it, I know.'

'Twelve years,' Abbie repeated thoughtfully. 'I hadn't realised.'

Bonnie nodded. 'I'm very fond of him, though what I feel is quite different to the way I felt about your father. I realise nothing would compare with that. But Don and I have a deep friendship, an understanding. We're comfortable together.' She paused. 'Not like you and Matt.' Her mother's remark was so casual that Abbie almost missed it. Then she met her mother's eyes and Bonnie nodded. 'A love made for lovers.'

Abbie swallowed, then sighed faintly. 'I didn't intend to fall in love, Mum. It happened almost without me knowing it. Matt slipped so effortlessly into my life.'

'Have you told him how you feel?' Bonnie asked.

'I've not really wanted to admit it to myself,' Abbie acknowledged as she stared at her mother's frowning expression. 'And what good would it do if I did? He's a young man and his whole future lies ahead of him—back in Adelaide. It was a fact I had to accept from the start.'

'But things can change, darling,' Bonnie argued gently. 'If it's the age gap you're concerned about, you're worrying unduly. As I've said, age makes no difference to true love.'

It was true that at first she had been conscious of the difference in their ages, but as they had grown to know one another better, age had seemed irrelevant. She realised what her mother said was relevant—if you fell in love with someone, age had little bearing on the relationship. Others might be aware of it, Abbie realised, but what did it matter if the two people involved knew how they felt about each other?

'Abbie, if Matt feels the same way,' Bonnie murmured, breaking into her thoughts, 'he won't want it to end either.'

Abbie paused, before speaking, then slowly shook her head. 'We agreed when we first started seeing each other that nothing could come of our relationship. We've discussed it since—recently, in fact. The situation hasn't changed. Matt has commitments in Australia, I have them here in England.'

'But practical commitments have no bearing for affairs of the heart,' Bonnie observed wryly.

Abbie looked down at her hands and nodded. 'I know that now. But when I met Matt I wasn't looking for a serious relationship. I suppose, after Sean, I hadn't expected to find what I have with Matt. As you said about Don, your relationship with him is different to the one you had with Dad.'

'It rather takes you by surprise, doesn't it?' Bonnie murmured with a small smile.

Abbie looked up. 'Yes, it does. Everything about my relationship with Matt has surprised me.'

Bonnie shook her head. 'But, darling, if you're in love with him, it doesn't have to end—'

Her comment was interrupted by the buzzing of Abbie's pager. As Abbie silenced it, she found that she was grateful for the natural pause in the conversation. Having made a call to the surgery, she slipped on her coat and returned to her mother who had taken the cups into the kitchen.

'It's Geraldine,' Abbie explained. 'She's on duty today and I told her to page me if she had any difficulties.'

'No trouble, I hope?' Bonnie set the china in the sink and turned to her daughter.

Abbie shrugged. 'It's Jasper, I'm afraid.'

Her mother nodded silently, then moved forward and reached out to hug her. 'Don't let your chance of happiness go, darling,' she whispered as she drew away.

These were words which remained in Abbie's mind as Bonnie accompanied her to the front door and waved good-bye. Abbie wondered as she drove away how it was possible that happiness had found her in such a short space of time and when she had least been expecting it. Perhaps it was only now, after her father's and Sean's deaths, that time had healed the emotional scars the tragedy had imposed. Whatever, there was no doubt in her mind that Matt had brought a joy to her life, a wonder and fulfilment that she could never have achieved without him.

However, once at Jasper's bedside, Abbie's mind was immediately brought back to the distress of her patient as Jasper struggled to breathe.

'It's respiratory problems,' said Geraldine quietly. 'I think he should be admitted. But I thought I should let you know first.'

Abbie examined her old friend who was, without doubt, suffering an infection of the breathing passages and lungs. The problem, often related to motor neurone disease, could result in further complications, and without hesitation she rang the hospital to arrange his admittance.

While they waited Marion packed a small case for

Jasper, and when the ambulance arrived Abbie relinquished her patient to the care of the paramedics.

Jasper was too ill to protest. Gently removed to a stretcher, he smiled at Marion. After the ambulance left, having said goodbye to Marion, Abbie and Geraldine walked to their cars.

Geraldine looked back at the house and frowned. 'Are Marion and Dave relatives of Mr Macdonald's?' she asked.

'No. Just tenants of the adjoining flat,' Abbie explained.

'She seemed very upset,' Geraldine commented. 'When is her baby due?'

'Late November.' Abbie smiled. 'You'll have chance to meet her properly next week when she comes to the clinic for her antenatal appointment.' Abbie hesitated. 'Are you happy with your flat?'

'It's lovely,' Geraldine replied enthusiastically. 'I can see the hills from my bedroom window, which is like waking up in a dream. I've always lived in crowded towns or cities. Now it really feels like the dream I've always had about living in the country has finally come true.'

Abbie arched an eyebrow. 'I was rather concerned about how you would take to rural life.'

Geraldine took a deep breath, inhaling the air in one deep gulp. 'Like a duck to water,' she said with a rueful grin. 'Though as to what Dr Carrig's patients think of me, we'll have to wait to see.' She shrugged. 'He'll be a hard act to follow. Almost everyone has said how sorry they are to see him go.'

Abbie nodded but said nothing, and Geraldine gave her a curious look as they parted. Matt's patients, Abbie reflected, weren't the only ones who would have a problem with his absence. Trying not to give way to the growing emptiness inside her, she drove home.

September's warm and sunlit days gradually gave way to crisp, cold mornings touched with early frost. October brought westerly winds and shook the leaves from the trees. The hills had turned dark and brooding and the caps of their summits were dusted in white.

Michele had her fifth birthday in early October, Matt his thirty-first. To Abbie's pain and pleasure, he joked that now he was closing the gap on her. *Did* love make age irrelevant? she wondered. Now, age no longer seemed to matter. What had concerned her once now seemed unimportant. It was, she realised, what people felt inside themselves that mattered.

Jasper seemed to improve in hospital. He was able to transfer from bed to chair or chair to bed and his fluid and electrolyte balance were maintained at positive levels. Marion and Dave were regular visitors and, despite the maintenance of a urinary catheter which Jasper disliked intensely, he appeared well enough to return home.

The day before his discharge, Abbie received a call from the hospital. The morning staff had arrived to discover his bed empty, a blanket rolled under his top cover to give the impression his bed was occupied. No one had seen him leave the ward and a search had been made of the hospital and the police informed.

Marion and Dave arrived at the surgery with Jonathan. 'He seemed well enough last night when we visited,' Dave said in bewilderment as they gathered in Abbie's room, trying to fathom out what could have happened. 'He was coming home tomorrow. We had everything planned.'

'Did he say anything at all unusual?' Matt asked as each of them struggled to think of a reason for Jasper's disappearance.

'Nothing,' sighed Marion, 'except it was suggested by the authorities that we would be helped with respite care for two weeks every three months. I did wonder if that upset him. But, with the baby coming, the hospital thought it would be the best way.'

'When was this?' asked Abbie.

'The day before yesterday, I think.' Marion bit her lip. 'If I'd realised he didn't want respite care, we could have thought of something else.'

'Did he have any outdoor clothing with him?' Matt asked.

Marion nodded. 'I told the police. A mac and a pair of trousers. And shoes, of course. He asked for them to be brought in. I didn't think anything of it at the time. Just that he was looking forward to coming home.'

'Maybe he's gone to see an old friend or something,' suggested Dave randomly.

It was then that Jonathan tugged his mother's sleeve. 'What about Trawsey, Mum?' he whispered shyly.

'Trawsey's a lake, darling,' Marion said, then looked up sharply at Abbie. 'Mr Macdonald was always telling Jonathan stories of the fish he caught in the lake. But why would he go there of all places?'

Abbie vaguely recalled the name of Trawsey. Her father and Jasper had fished there many years ago as young men. 'It's probably worth mentioning to the police,' she said quietly. 'I'd better do it.'

Leaving the room to walk to the office where she could dial an outside line in privacy, some sixth sense told her that Jonathan might have given them the clue to Jasper's disappearance.

A body was discovered twenty four hours later on the banks of Trawsey Lake and was later identified by Frank Morgan who elected to go to the mortuary and carry out the grim task. Jasper's heart had failed some hours before, it was revealed, his frail body unable to take the exposure to the elements on a cold, frostbitten night.

A taxi driver came forward to explain that a man answering Jasper's description had called for a taxi from a phone booth near the hospital. He had told the driver he had been to an old boys' reunion and that his condition was caused by a little over-indulgence. Until the man had heard the news of Jasper's discovery on the cab radio he had thought no more about the unusual fare.

How Jasper had managed to walk to the lake from the place where he had been dropped by the taxi remained a mystery, but Abbie felt that his determination would have triumphed over his physical disability. She would not have been surprised if he had tried to attempt the hills, but the climb would have been impossible. It stood to reason, therefore, that Jasper had chosen Trawsey Lake and his own form of respite at the close of his life.

Jasper's funeral took place the week before Matt left. The best part of Rendale filled the church and the church hall afterwards. Though Jasper had been a recluse for the past year, the circumstances of his death had touched the small community.

Matt, Abbie and Frank attended the hour-long service, while Geraldine remained on duty at the surgery. Frank stayed on at the reception afterwards, but Matt and Abbie returned to the practice.

It was a day that could have come straight from summer—golden trees and glistening sun and a cloudless sky. 'As Jasper would have liked it to be,' Matt commented as he drove Abbie through Rendale.

'I hope he didn't suffer,' Abbie said quietly. 'He must have been so cold.'

Matt reached out to squeeze her hand. 'He made his choice and, from what we can gather, the end came swiftly.'

Abbie nodded, staring from the window as the houses and cottages passed by. The world was continuing as normal, life going on. She felt a deep sadness and sense of loss, but she also felt relief for Jasper. He would have hated to have been a burden on anyone. 'I'm glad you knew him,' she said softly.

Matt nodded. 'I'll miss those games of backgammon.'

'He liked you,' Abbie said, clearing her throat.

Matt turned to look at her. 'One of the last things he told me was that I should take care of you.'

She met his gaze and for an instant wondered what his thoughts were. How could she tell him how she yearned with all her heart to be cared for and loved, knowing that she would be placing him in an impossible position if she did so? His future had been carved out long before she had known him. No doubt, in six months' time, when he would be enjoying the life that he was destined for, he might occasionally recall the happiness they had shared together this summer.

Her moment of indecision passed swiftly as a horn blared behind them and an impatient driver claimed Matt's full attention. Abbie returned her gaze to the October houses bathed in golden sunshine.

That evening they took Michele for a walk by the river while Joely and Phil drove out into the country for dinner. Michele was in high spirits and told them of the new friends she was making at school and the ballet that she and Lucy had been selected to dance in at Christmas.

'We're in the chorus,' Michele explained as they crossed the river to the thatched pub on the opposite side of the road. 'It's really not a Christmas ballet but Miss Murilova says that it doesn't matter. The parents will like it anyway.'

Michele paused as they reached the flight of steps leading to the terrace. 'Watch me, Uncle Matt. This is first position, this is second and this is third.' Pointing her toes and spreading her arms, Michele demonstrated.

Matt applauded. 'Is that what you do in the chorus?'

Michele giggled as they strolled into the children's room. 'No, we do cor-core—'

'Choreographed dances?' Abbie suggested.

Michele nodded. 'Will you come to see me, Uncle Matt? I'm one of the elves. So is Lucy.'

Abbie glanced at him as they sat at one of the small white tables. He met her gaze fleetingly as they settled themselves on the chairs. 'When is your ballet, Michele?'

'December the fifteenth at seven o'clock.' Michele looked at him expectantly. 'Mummy said she can get free tickets for everyone, even Grandma and Grandpa Don. And Uncle Matt can sit next to Uncle Phil.'

'I'd like that very much,' Matt replied, adding reluctantly, 'But I might not be here, Michele. Aunt Abbie will have to take my place.'

Michele's small, round face dropped. 'Where are you going?'

'Back home,' Matt said quietly. 'To Australia.'

'But I thought this was your home,' Michele persisted. 'Mummy says you were born in England.'

'Yes, I was.' Matt glanced at Abbie and raised his dark eyebrows. 'Look, why don't I go and get the drinks? Then you can show us some more of your ballet steps.'

Michele and Abbie watched him walk away, his tall figure disappearing between the tables. Michele left her chair and stood by Abbie, frowning as she drew circles on the table with her finger. 'Aunt Abbie, I thought Uncle Matt would be here for ever. I don't want him to go away. He's really nice. Why does he have to go?'

Abbie pulled her niece onto her knee and brushed her fringe from her eyes. 'Because he's a doctor in Australia,' she said.

'Why can't he be a doctor in England?'

'Well, he has for a little while.'

'Doesn't he like it here?'

'Of course he does.'

'Then why can't he stay?'

Abbie buried her face in Michele's sweet-smelling hair, attempting to hide the emotion that was filling her and which she did not want Michele to see. But it was too late. Michele eased herself away and looked gravely at her aunt.

'Do you love Uncle Matt, Aunt Abbie?'

'I'm very fond of him, darling.' Abbie smiled, trying to avoid Michele's intent stare.

'I think he loves you.'

'What makes you say that?'

'Oh, I just know. And, anyway, he lives with you. He wouldn't like living with anyone else. And he's Uncle Phil's best friend. And Grandma likes him and I like him and Lucy likes him.'

If only it were as simple, Abbie thought as she hugged Michele against her. That childlike sense of logic was sometimes so honest that it was astonishing. But it was impossible to explain the complications that adults made for themselves, the relationship between her and Matt apparently straightforward to Michele's young mind.

'Why don't you show me some more of your dance?' Abbie suggested, attempting to divert Michele's train of thought.

Michele hesitated. 'Maybe later,' she murmured, then frowned at the group of children who came running into the play area. She slipped from Abbie's knee to watch them.

Matt returned with a tray of drinks—orange squash for Michele, a glass of white wine for Abbie and a shandy for himself. The crisps, Abbie suspected, were meant to divert Michele's attention, and to that end they worked as she saw the unexpected treat.

Very soon, taking her crisps with her, she began to play

with the other children on the colourful wooden amusements.

'I hate to disappoint her like that,' Matt said after a while, and Abbie nodded.

'Children are resilient. She understands.' Abbie sipped her drink, unable to look at Matt directly. A silence developed between them as Abbie watched Michele, the questions that her niece had asked her going round in her mind. There were no answers to Michele's questions, in fact, for ironically they were the questions that Abbie had been asking herself. Not that she would dream of repeating them to Matt. If he had been in any doubt at all about leaving then his reply to Michele tonight had shown that he had no uncertainty about returning to Australia.

Eventually Michele tired of her activities with the other children and yawning, came to sit in between Abbie and Matt, her eyes sleepy.

'Time to walk home,' Abbie said as Michele finished her drink.

'Can Uncle Matt read me a bedtime story?' she wanted to know.

'Yes, if it's not too late when we get home.' Abbie glanced at Matt. They met each other's eyes and Matt nodded, reaching out to lift Michele into his arms.

'How about a piggyback?' he teased, and, giggling, Michele nodded.

It was a more cheerful walk home, the gloomy moment in the children's room at the pub forgotten. Once at the cottage, Abbie organised Michele into her nightly routine and very soon Michele was tucked up in bed. The story topic was elves and fairies once more and Abbie listened to Matt's deep, rich tones as he read to Michele until she fell asleep.

Finding her way around Joely's kitchen, Abbie set supper out on trays, adding fruit to cheese, freshly baked bread and hot soup. Matt caught hold of her wrist and turned her towards him, his expression hungry as his lips closed over hers.

Her response was swift as her arms went around his neck and she closed her eyes, surrendering to the physical need that ached within her. For a while they remained in one another's arms, eager to resolve whatever barrier had been erected between them.

Finally they sat, spreading the food before them on the coffee-table in the cosy warmth of Joely's front room, the unhappy subject of Matt's departure for the moment forgotten.

It wasn't an easy week. To compound the nausea which still beset her each morning, the evenings that she shared with Matt were touched with poignant shadows. Small things she would remember after he was gone—their shared meals, their walks in the evenings, the cups of tea at the crack of dawn when either of them returned from a house call.

Each morning they got up and went into surgery, she in the Fiesta, he in the Citroën. Each day presented last-minute memories that Abbie was hoarding away until the time came when she was alone—when it was over.

Like the morning she was so preoccupied she left the house wearing two different shoes, or the morning when Matt dropped the box of cornflakes and each separate flake seemed to find its own route across the kitchen floor.

On their final evening they went to bed and lay beside each other, words unnecessary as they made love. The emotion had risen into her throat, almost choking her. Tears, which she had firmly withheld for the past week, flowed and he smoothed them away with his finger, kissing her damp cheeks. She had tried not to let him see her distress.

She had vowed to accept the inevitable but that meant nothing as she clung to him.

Only the morning brought a strange kind of relief. Matt showered and dressed and quietly slipped away. Abbie, numb and empty, remained in their bed, afraid to speak or move.

Phil's car engine purred outside the house in the early light. Abbie lay there, listening for the front door to open and close as it had so many times over the months before, knowing that every creak on the stairs, every squeak and rattle, was the last squeak, the last rattle, they would share together.

The final sounds came. The slow, soft rush of cold morning air into the hall. The click of the lock, the lift of the latch. Her heart racing as she measured each of Matt's strides down the garden path. A car moving off...and silence. Only then was it finally over.

CHAPTER TWELVE

ON THE first day of November Abbie was woken by the ringing of her bedside telephone. It was, according to her watch, just gone eight a.m. The voice that came over the line as she sat up in bed was just recognisable as Geraldine's. The very next sensation was one of her stomach revolving and, swinging her legs to the floor, she took a breath before she spoke.

'Sorry to phone so early,' apologised Geraldine a few moments later, 'but I've got an horrendous cold. I think it's the flu.'

'Don't worry,' Abbie said, lifting her head as the room spun. 'I'll take the calls today.'

'Have you got a pager?' Geraldine asked.

'Yes…a spare one. I'll activate it and let Frank know I'm on call.'

Geraldine went into a fit of sneezing. When she had stopped she apologised once again and Abbie told her to stay in bed.

After replacing the phone, Abbie sat quietly and waited for her stomach to settle as she pulled her robe around her. Sometimes, if she was lucky, the nausea abated, returning occasionally during the day, but this morning it seemed to have taken a hold and she went to the bathroom, her forehead bathed in perspiration.

Sitting on the edge of the bath, she held a cool flannel to her cheeks. It certainly wasn't flu—the attacks had been too consistent. She stared bleakly at the walls. She had chosen to stay on at the cottage—the rent was settled until Christmas. It had just seemed like the best thing to do at the time. Perhaps the only thing to do. Bonnie had suggested she go home, but Abbie knew that she could never return now. This was home. This was where she had begun to live again.

Cautiously she lifted her head and took slow steps to the basin, where she ran the cold water. Rinsing the flannel, she drew it across her face and took a deep breath, hoping that the nausea was a figment of her imagination, ignoring the voice inside her which told her the true cause of the problem.

She padded from the bathroom across to the window. The morning was breathtaking—white with frost, clear blue sky. The road outside glistened and sparkled in the weak sunshine.

Day number three since Matt's plane had flown out of Heathrow. Day number four since he had walked out of the front door for the last time. How many days, she wondered, before she stopped counting?

A wave of sickness engulfed her again. Unable to ignore the duty she must perform, she returned to the bathroom and made the test. A short while later she was sitting on the end of her bed, her thoughts in turmoil.

When could it have happened? When had she conceived? She tried to think calmly, recalling the first time she and Matt had made love. They had taken a chance, yes. She could have understood if she had conceived then. But she had taken the morning-after pill and fortunately there had been no developments.

After that she had gone on the Pill. Abbie fought back another wave of nausea, trying to think. Then she searched her handbag for her diary and discovered that she had changed the brand of Pill she was taking around the time of Bonnie's surprise dinner party. After that she had had a period. However, it had not been, she recalled, a full period. For a few days she had felt out of sorts. In August her system had seemed to return to normal. But she had missed the next period and she had decided to stop the Pill. Matt had then taken precautions…

She closed her diary and stood up. Could she be as much as three months pregnant? It was highly unlikely but, then, her system had been in upheaval. Torn between her emotions, Abbie's reaction of disbelief soon faded as she cast her mind back. Had she unconsciously suppressed what she had known was happening to her? Had she known all this time that she was pregnant, dismissing it because Matt was leaving?

Confused, she stood up, focused her mind on the day ahead and took her pager from a drawer. Phoning Frank to let him know that she had taken Geraldine's call, she summoned her depleted energy and took a shower.

Dressed in jeans and a warm sweater, one of Matt's blue-and-white striped rugby shirts, she resisted the urge to bury her face in the soft material. She could bring his presence back when she smelt him but at this moment, she needed to think, to decide what she was going to do.

A baby. Six months from now. April. A spring baby. Her heart fluttered and she swallowed. *Her* baby. The baby that she had wanted for so long. A part of Matt and a part of her, laying curled in her stomach, partially formed, depending on her for survival.

Of course, she must do a second test, but she knew— deep inside her she knew—that life was growing. Life that she and Matt had created with love. A sudden flow of pleasure went through her, a wonder and joy. Then, almost as soon as it filled her, so too did dismay, then fear.

Fear that she was going to bear a child and raise it without a father. A father whom she loved and had let go. Could she do it? Could she bear to have that happen? But what other choice was there? To tell Matt? To put him in a position where he would be unable to refuse her?

How many times had she seen relationships break up because of that? Would she want him to abandon his career and his life on the other side of the world because she had fallen pregnant? Could she live with that for the rest of her life, never knowing if, through conscience alone, he had returned to support her? She also had to consider whether she could give up her life and go to him—but what if he didn't want her?

There had been more between them, surely? But—and the thought devastated her—he had never said he loved her. It was then that Abbie knew what she was going to do. She would have her baby, give birth to the precious life growing within her. She was appalled at the thought of having to tell her mother, who had already had to face Joely's pregnancy. Even worse, what would Joely's and Michele's reactions be?

Abbie took a deep breath, knowing it would be hard on them all—as though history were repeating itself. But this was her child, her long-awaited child, and somehow she would see her way through.

While she was attempting to sip her first glass of water and nibble a biscuit, the phone rang again. She thought it was probably Geraldine, having forgotten to mention something, but the voice that came over the line wasn't Geraldine's.

'You'd better come,' growled Donovan Kilerne. 'She's got them pains again.'

'Donovan?' Abbie asked, alert now and frowning into the mouthpiece. 'What's wrong?'

'Pains,' he said again, then added, 'We got no truck. You'll have to come here.'

'Is Gwyneth in labour?' Abbie asked. 'Where are you phoning from?'

'The farm down the road,' Donovan replied, then the line went dead.

Overcoming the waves of nausea, Abbie phoned Frank and explained where she was going.

'When is the Donovans' baby due?' he asked.

'At the end of November.' Abbie hoped that conditions on Esk Fell would remain calm. There seemed to be no wind outside and the sun was growing stronger. 'Will you take any local calls while I'm away?'

Frank assured her he would and, locking the cottage after her, Abbie set off in the Fiesta. Her thoughts returned to her own baby as she drove. Would the knowledge that she was carrying Matt's child help her to bear his absence? Or, as time went on, would it work in reverse?

Making an effort to adapt, she had struggled through each day after Matt's departure. Attempting to function as normal, she had dragged herself home at night to an unreal, empty world. Now she mustn't cry for the child inside her must be loved and cherished.

Sooner than she expected, Abbie realised she had arrived at the foot of Esk Fell. It loomed above her as the car started its upward climb. Matt had been with her last time, she recalled. Matt had reached out to hold her hand, supported her through that stormy night.

Almost as though she felt his presence in the car, she drove on, reaching the bend in the road that had claimed Sean's and her father's lives. The sadness was still there but dulled and distant. Had she finally come to terms with Esk Fell's unhappy history?

Abbie felt the familiar pop of her eardrums as the car climbed higher. Passing the isolated cottage that Jasper had phoned from, she peered through mist that always surrounded the summit. Rounding the next corner, the slate roof of the Kilernes' cottage twinkled through.

Minutes later she came face to face with Donovan Kilerne. He answered her knock and she entered, finding the cottage dark and cold.

'How is Gwyneth?' Abbie asked.

She received a grunt for reply as he pointed towards the fire. Gwyneth Kilerne, stretched out on a makeshift bed by the hearth, was attempting to push her child into the world. Between them they managed to get Gwyneth into the bedroom. As Gwyneth collapsed on the bed Abbie shouted for towels and hot water, and Donovan, waking from his trance, hurried off.

Abbie washed her hands in the basin beside the bed and spread the plastic sheeting over the covers. 'The baby's head is coming, Gwyneth,' Abbie explained calmly. 'I want you to pant and stop pushing.'

'Donnie!' Gwyneth called.

Donovan, delivering the hot water, wore an expression of sheer fright on his face.

Seconds later the baby's face appeared. Abbie cleared the filmy membrane which covered the miniature features. As she supported the tiny shoulders, she saw that the cord was looped around the baby's neck.

'They'll die,' she heard Donovan whisper. But Abbie had no time to respond as she looped the cord gently over the baby's head. As its tiny shoulders emerged, silence hung in the room. Gwyneth stopped crying and stared at her silent baby. Donovan was frozen to the spot.

Abbie wiped the baby's mouth with a sterile cloth and lowered the tiny head downwards to drain away the mucus. It seemed an eternity, but as Abbie wiggled the five tiny toes he yelled loudly, his fists flailing in the air.

Abbie met Donovan's astonished stare. 'You have a beautiful baby son,' she said softly. 'Congratulations.' Lifting the child away from the birth canal, she handed him to Gwyneth.

It was then, as she glanced back, she saw that Donovan was weeping. Slipping her arm around his stiff shoulders, she steered him towards the bed. Donovan sank to his knees, gratefully embracing his wife and newborn son.

Abbie emerged into the crisp November morning. The sun had broken through the mist and the frost had melted. It was a glorious November day. She heaved a sigh, feeling as though she had run an emotional marathon. The last half-hour she had spent with the Kilernes had answered many questions. If only Matt had been here to tell the story to…

Despair hit her. Like a blow to the stomach she realised that this was only the beginning. There would be many times in the future when she needed him, craved his comfort and warmth, physically and mentally.

She walked to the car, the beautiful sun-filled morning shimmering around her. All this, and the void inside her—the stark realisation that her life would never be complete without Matt.

'Abbie?'

She looked up, turned her head, and saw nothing but the white-topped peaks in the distance and a bird flying overhead in the clear blue sky. Now she was imagining things. She wanted him so much, missed him so much, that she was hearing his voice, that deep, wonderful tone that was still in her head days after he had gone.

'Abbie?' There it was again, the voice she knew so well that lived continually in her mind. Her heart pounded as she reached out to steady herself against the car. Someone gripped her shoulder and she turned, her eyes unable to believe what was in front of her.

'Abbie, are you all right?' He supported her as she almost fell against him. 'Darling, you're so pale—what's wrong?'

All she could do was shake her head as he opened the car door and lowered her gently to the seat. 'Frank told me you were up here. I've left the car at the gate—I didn't know whether I might have missed you.' He dropped on one knee, frowning up into her face. 'Abbie—speak to me.'

It couldn't be, she thought as the feeling of faintness threatened to overwhelm her. It just wasn't possible. Here, in front of her, his dark eyes shining down at her, his hair running softly into her fingers as she lifted her hands and touched its thickness. Solid muscle, skin and bone. The warm jacket he had bought recently in Hobcraig, the jeans and boots he had worn on the day he departed.

And then his lips were on hers, his mouth opening hers as she leaned forward and allowed herself a sigh that travelled up from way down inside her. Only when she realised that Donovan Kilerne was standing watching them did she convince herself that Matt was real.

Matt looked around and stood up. 'Hello, Donovan.'

The older man nodded, frowning at them curiously. 'You all right, missus?' he said to Abbie.

She nodded, and rose slowly to her feet, holding onto the car door for support. 'Yes, I'm fine, thank you.' She looked at Matt. 'Donovan has a son. He's beautiful. Why don't you go and have a look at him?'

Matt gazed at her for a moment, his expression uncertain, but she nodded again and gestured to the open door. 'I just need a little fresh air. Go on, I'll wait for you.'

'You'd better,' he said softly. 'Sit down until I come back.'

She did as she was told, and watched the tall figure of Matt enter the house, Donovan following.

For a moment she sat quite still. The air flowed into her nostrils and revived her, the sickness fading. Matt was here. He had kissed her, touched her. He wasn't a figment of her imagination. Some miracle had brought him back.

It was a long time before she began breathing normally, her heart still racing as she tried to compose herself and prepare for the sight of Matt walking out of the door and coming towards her.

The moment eventually came. Smiling, Matt talked for a few moments to Donovan before he closed the door behind him. With long strides he came towards her, his breath curling up into the cold morning air.

She stood to greet him, her eyes filling with tears. For whatever reason he had returned, there was one thing she knew for certain. Destiny had brought him back to her. To her—and their child. This time there would be no secrets between them…

They lay in bed, the afternoon light coming through the window, Abbie's pager propped against a book on her bedside table. 'I love you, Abbie, I love you with all my heart,' Matt whispered. 'Why didn't you tell me?' he asked softly. 'How long had you been feeling sick in the mornings?'

Guiltily she looked up at him. 'For some while,' she admitted.

'Then you must have known… Why did you keep it to yourself? Abbie—*our baby, our child*!'

'I wasn't sure,' she answered as, gazing into his eyes, she saw how wrong she would have been not to have told him. 'I only took the test this morning.'

'Would you have told me?'

She lowered her eyes, unable to meet his perceptive gaze.

'Abbie, don't you know what this baby means to me? Don't you understand how much I want this child?'

She shook her head, her voice unsteady as she spoke. 'You have everything waiting for you back in Australia. A career, a life—'

'And what would it be without you? Without our son or daughter. Abbie, we are a family now. Do you realise that?'

She could hardly believe that it was true. She was still

trying to convince herself that she had just made love to a real man. Her man. Her baby's father.

'All those months, all I wanted was for you to ask me to stay,' he whispered against her cheek. 'That was all I wanted.'

'But we had an arrangement—'

'And I thought you were determined to keep it.'

'But I couldn't ask you to give it all up for me. How could I have lived with that? You might have been unhappy and unfulfilled. You might have come to have so many regrets.'

'Do you honestly believe that?' He lifted her chin and gazed into her eyes. 'Didn't you know that I was in love with you?'

'Oh, Matt…' She looked up at him uncertainly. 'If only I had allowed myself to believe that.'

'I was a fool. I should have opened my heart to you.'

'Why didn't you?'

'Because I thought that was what you wanted. I thought you valued your life as it was. I felt I had no place in your future.'

'What made you change your mind?'

'When we got to London and Phil dropped me at the airport I sat there for hours, just thinking. Suddenly I knew I could never get on that plane. I booked into a hotel. I picked up the phone a dozen times. I even wrote and screwed up the letter. Then finally I knew I had to come back to tell you how I felt. I had to look into your eyes and tell you…'

'Oh, Matt… I just thought we…that we had agreed—'

'I asked you if you needed to be taken care of—do you remember, after Jasper's funeral?'

She nodded. 'I didn't know whether you were serious. I wondered if you might have someone in Adelaide.'

'Abbie, tell me you love me,' he said softly. 'I must hear you say it.'

She kissed him slowly, inhaling the aroma that was no longer a dream or a memory but as real as the firm muscle and bone that moved beneath her fingers. 'I love you Matt. We love you.'

'Oh, God, Abbie, to think we almost—'

She lifted her fingers and placed them on his lips. 'Don't say it. Somehow we would have known.'

'That's all I need to hear.'

Lifting her face, she took a breath and placed his hands on her stomach, looking into his eyes as she did so. 'Our baby, my darling, our child.'

'Our beautiful child,' he whispered with eyes that looked back at her with desire.

It was later, when the evening shadows had filled the tiny bedroom and Abbie lay comfortably in the strong arms of the man she loved, her body replete with happiness.

'I've been wondering,' Matt said, pulling her against him, 'if I can summon up the courage to ask for my old job back. I'm prepared to wait until a vacancy arises.' His voice was soft as he bent his head and whispered, 'You never know what the future holds.'

'I've a fair idea,' she murmured, closing her eyes and imagining the small, precious bundle that would lie in her arms. 'You won't have to wait long,' she assured him. 'Does six months sound about right to you?'

'Sounds good to me,' he said as she turned to kiss him. 'Now, while we're on the subject of dates, we've one more to consider. And, in view of our busy schedule, I would suggest we make it pretty soon.'

'Finding somewhere to live with enough bedrooms?' she guessed innocently, but he was already shaking his head.

'That comes a long way down the line.'

'Well, it's Christmas next month and Joely's getting married…'

'Warmer.' He grinned. Taking her into his arms, he whispered, 'One more guess.'

But words were unnecessary as they looked into one another's eyes. Heaven had sent him back to her and heaven would take care of the rest.

MILLS & BOON®

*M*akes
any time
special

Enjoy a romantic novel from
Mills & Boon®

Presents...   *Enchanted*™   TEMPTATION.

Historical Romance™   **⊣MEDICAL ROMANCE**

MILLS & BOON®

MEDICAL ROMANCE™

GOOD HUSBAND MATERIAL by Sheila Danton

Rebecca Groom soon realises how attractive she finds the senior partner, Dr Marc Johnson. But the surgery intends to expand, using an old house that holds dear memories for Rebecca...

ALWAYS MY VALENTINE by Leah Martyn

Charge Nurse Geena Wilde liked Dr Jack O'Neal very much, but it wasn't until Valentine's Day that Geena received a gorgeous bunch of red roses from Jack, and an invitation to the Valentine Ball! That was a *very* good beginning...

COURTING DR CADE by Josie Metcalfe

Damon and Katherine were instant friends. Now Katherine's grandmother will lose her beloved home unless Katherine is married by Leap Year's day! But a simple marriage of convenience turns into something far more complicated!

A FAMILY CONCERN by Margaret O'Neill

For Gemma Fellows and her six-year-old daughter, Daisy, the cottage is a godsend. It's a new start—and as far as Dr Sam Mallory is concerned, Gemma and Daisy are perfect for him...

Available from 4th February 2000

Available at most branches of WH Smith, Tesco, Martins, Borders, Easons, Volume One/James Thin and most good paperback bookshops

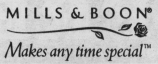

4 FREE

books and a surprise gift!

We would like to take this opportunity to thank you for reading this Mills & Boon® book by offering you the chance to take FOUR more specially selected titles from the Medical Romance™ series absolutely FREE! We're also making this offer to introduce you to the benefits of the Reader Service™—

★ FREE home delivery
★ FREE gifts and competitions
★ FREE monthly Newsletter
★ Exclusive Reader Service discounts
★ Books available before they're in the shops

Accepting these FREE books and gift places you under no obligation to buy, you may cancel at any time, even after receiving your free shipment. Simply complete your details below and return the entire page to the address below. *You don't even need a stamp!*

YES! Please send me 4 free Medical Romance books and a surprise gift. I understand that unless you hear from me, I will receive 6 superb new titles every month for just £2.40 each, postage and packing free. I am under no obligation to purchase any books and may cancel my subscription at any time. The free books and gift will be mine to keep in any case.

M0EA

Ms/Mrs/Miss/Mr ....Initials................................
                                         BLOCK CAPITALS PLEASE
Surname ....

Address ....

....

....Postcode................................

Send this whole page to:
UK: FREEPOST CN81, Croydon, CR9 3WZ
EIRE: PO Box 4546, Kilcock, County Kildare (stamp required)

MILLS & BOON®

Coming in January 2000...

ACCIDENT AND EMERGENCY

Three exciting stories based in the casualty departments of busy hospitals. Meet the staff who juggle an active career and still find time for romance and the patients who depend on their care to reach a full recovery.

Three of your favourite authors:

Caroline Anderson

Josie Metcalfe

Sharon Kendrick

Available at most branches of WH Smith, Tesco, Martins, Borders, Easons, Volume One / James Thin and most good paperback bookshops